About Cop On Her Doorstep

In the six years since her husband was killed by S.W.A.T., Carrie Padilla has spent long hours at work, rebuilding a life for herself and her son. The little time she has at home is spent keeping her eight-year-old son out of trouble, but he is all too eager to try to be the man in the house. When a handsome cop shows up on her doorstep, her errant son in tow, Carrie's heart stutters. The sexy Italian cop sets off all kinds of bells in her system, and she knows there's only one thing she can do to save what is left of her family, her husband's memory, and her heart...avoid her new neighbor at all costs.

S.W.A.T. officer Jake Stafani already lost one little boy to gang violence, the dead boy's older brother is missing, and Jake's not about to let the same thing happen to a neighbor's son. He drags the youngster home only to discover much more than just a passing interest in the boy's beautiful, but wary, mother. Forced to take a leave of absence after a bust goes awry, Jake can think of nothing better to occupy his time than to keep Carrie and her son safe until the missing boy is found. That missing young man holds the key to taking the gang off the streets, and keeping Carrie's son safe, once and for all.

But Jake doesn't count on the passion that flares between them, or on his stubborn but beautiful neighbor distracting him from his job. He doesn't expect her amazing son to steal a piece of his heart. Jake is ready to risk everything for Carrie, body and soul. But it's not all up to him. If their new love is to survive, Carrie will need to be strong enough to see the man's beating heart behind the badge, to look beyond the pain of her past, and decide that loving again is worth the risk.

Cop On Her Doorstep

By Karen Docter

A True Love In Uniform Novel

Contemporary Romance

© 2015 by Karen Docter

Dedication

This book, and all of the books that follow in the *True Love In Uniform* Series, are dedicated to the men and women in uniform who are doing it right every day.

Thank you.

Stay safe!

Chapter One

"What do you mean you're taking me off the streets?" Jake Stefani stared at Captain Julian Monroe, still reeling over the reaming he'd received from his S.W.A.T. commander minutes earlier. His day hit the express chute into the shit-can more than three hours ago with a bust that had gone sideways, and it looked like it wasn't finished yet. "Tell me you're not sticking me behind a desk."

"I'm taking you off the streets completely. You're officially on vacation," he glanced down at his watch, "now."

No way! "How long?"

"Four weeks."

Adrenaline, dread, *something* nasty spiked in Jake's chest. He pushed it down. Different tactics were in order. "C'mon, Uncle Jules, you're overreacting. I'll take a couple of days off if you insist, but be reason—"

His uncle slammed a palm down on the desk. "It'll be a month under house arrest if you don't shut up, Jake. I'll be damned if I'm going to explain to your mother why her only son's being returned to her in a body bag. She'll serve my head in one of her tureen bowls, and my Francesca will help her."

In the seven years since leaving the smaller police force in Colorado Springs, Colorado in favor of the larger one in the metro-Denver suburb of Riverton, Jake and his uncle had been careful to keep their family and work relationships separated. The genuine concern reflected in his boss's expression did more to defuse Jake's anger than words could. "I doubt Zia Francesca would side with her sister against her husband," he said, "no matter what the issue."

"Then you've learned nothing about the protective instincts of the Mazzotti women. Maybe I'll sic them on you, let them knock sense into that hard head of yours. The psych doc's about given up trying to chase you down."

There was some good news! Since coming on board in February, the police psychologist had dogged Jake's footsteps like a thirteen-year-old groupie on a boy band. He'd been hard-pressed to keep his hands off the man's scrawny neck. Suspecting where this vacation idea had originated, he regretted not giving in to his baser impulses. "That quack couldn't fix a broken toilet seat with a roll of duct tape and instructions written by a four-year-old," he said. "There's nothing wrong with me."

"Your last evaluation says that's not precisely an accurate statement." His uncle snorted. "Of course, he gave more than half the force the same evaluation so I'm inclined to question some of his findings."

The disgust lining his voice sliced the tension between them, and Jake relaxed back in his seat for the first time since entering his superior's office. "Only some of those findings?"

"Still having those nightmares?"

The muscles between his shoulder blades drew tight again. Damn. He should never have shared the specter of the recurrent nightmares with his uncle in a weak moment over one too many beers. He'd handed the man more ammunition to push him into what amounted to a poorly disguised administrative leave.

"Haven't had one in a long time."

Three weeks was a long time when he'd dreamed almost nightly the first two months after the kid he'd befriended in his old neighborhood was killed. He'd tried to help Mateo Reyes to extricate himself from the SKL Dragons—the Skyline Street gang he'd joined alongside his sixteen-year-old brother on Riverton's west side—without success. The ten-year-old had died in his arms after the Dragons cornered him in the alley behind their apartment building. If Jake hadn't put the kid off when he'd asked for help, Mateo might still be alive.

His uncle didn't call him on his half-truth. "Tell me about the S.W.A.T. incident."

"You haven't read the report?"

"Tell me what's missing."

Something about the demand told Jake to tread carefully. His reports were always meticulous. The man was excavating for something. "I screwed up. Every last detail of my screw up is in the report. In triplicate. In your files. In the S.W.A.T. files. In the psych doc's office, too, I'm betting. What more do you want me to say?"

"I want you to admit the drug dealer got the drop on you because you were distracted by the thought Jesus Garza was in that crack house."

The accusation ran too near the mark. "Since we knew going in it was a SKL operation, there was every reason to assume one or more of the leaders were inside." Finding the Dragon "chairman" would have been a bonus as far as Jake was concerned. "That isn't the reason the bust wasn't the clean insertion we'd planned. I swear I heard something. It drew me off point before the rest of the team was in place."

"Salazar was right beside you when you entered the premises. He didn't hear anything."

He already knew what was in Salazar's report. It didn't change the fact that some instinct pulled Jake off target, an instinct that had ultimately saved his life. There might be an ongoing discussion about his preemptive movement alerting the gangbangers too soon, that gunfire could have been avoided, but he knew the truth. If he hadn't moved, it would have been his head exploding in a hail of bullets instead of the wall behind where he'd stood seconds earlier.

His captain frowned. "Look, Jake, I get it. You want retribution for the Reyes kid. But you can't be focused on punching holes in SKL to the exclusion of everything else. It's my responsibility to keep everyone under my command in tiptop shape, physically and mentally."

Jake worked out regularly in the station gym, so he knew it wasn't his physical performance under fire here. "So this is administrative leave," he said.

"Call it whatever you want," he retorted. "You have four weeks saved up and I want you to take them. The only way I see that happening is if I force the issue.

"It's not too late to go fishing with your cousins at Lake Powell. Gino and Lorenzo aren't leaving for a couple of days and they'd love to throw an extra pole on the boat for you." When Jake said nothing, he continued. "You could fly to Italy and spend some time with the Stefani-Mazzotti family. It's been seven years since your great-grandfather's funeral and you haven't been back." He paused, and then took another tack. "You could go to Kansas City and track down that girlfriend of yours.

Fix whatever went wrong between you. That would make your mother happy."

No way was Jake heading back to Italy anytime soon. If he thought Mama was bad with her incessant matchmaking, she was a neophyte compared to the women he ran into that one trip. There were more single women at his great-grandfather's funeral than lived in the four nearest villages. Just thinking about it damn near made him shake in his boots.

As for his ex-girlfriend? He wasn't throwing his neck on that chopping block again. One of these days he'd have to tell his family what really went wrong between him and Daniela. *Or maybe not.* "You think I can simply skip town or go fishing while the SKL does whatever they want?"

"I should've forced this leave months ago," his uncle muttered. He dragged his hand over his face. "You have to let go of your guilt, Jake. You're holding on too tight and it's interfering with your job."

That pricked his pride. "I'm damn good at my job."

"You're so damned good you almost got yourself killed three hours ago!"

With a glance at the functional gray wall clock, Jake took a deep breath to fight off the enervating effect of his second double shift of the week. Four-thirty a.m. It had been an overlong dogwatch, the S.W.A.T. incident in question had been a cluster, and his king-size bed sounded more and more tempting.

"Look," he dug for calm, "the banger missed. He was so doped up on his own product he couldn't hit the broadside of a barn. I can accept that you want to pull me off the streets for a day or two, but can't we shelve this discussion until tomorrow?"

"That banger might have been high enough to sing to the angels, but he didn't shoot at a barn. He aimed at your thick skull. A two-inch margin of error is not okay, and we are not shelving this. You won't be here tomorrow."

"Please, Uncle Jules." Jake wasn't comfortable begging, but desperation clawed at his insides. "I'll work a desk. I'll sleep on a cot in a broom closet if that's what it takes."

"No. It's done." He stood, his indication the conversation was terminated whether his subordinate was finished or not. "Take this break. Decompress. When you return, we'll discuss your future here."

Wait. When did this morning's incident become a threat to his career? No matter how much the team trained for every contingency, shit happened.

Jake bolted to his feet. "This job is my life. I can't sit on my thumbs for two days, let alone thirty."

"Then find some nice drop-dead gorgeous woman and spend the entire month in bed if that's what you need to keep your head down." His uncle walked to the door, opened the door and held up a hand in warning when Jake opened his mouth. "Just stay out of trouble. If I see your face around here one second before your vacation is up, I'll toss your career right out the nearest window. Do you hear me?"

Unable to believe he meant to enforce this edict, Jake walked to the doorway. "The entire precinct heard you, Captain," he said tightly.

"Good." His superior scowled at the quiet squad room over Jake's shoulder. "Then everyone knows not to take on trouble by talking to you before you come back, especially about anything regarding police work.

The shop is not open to you for the duration."

"Captain—"

"Enjoy your vacation, Stefani. That's an order." He motioned him out of his office and shut the door with a resounding click.

Jake's irritation grew when he saw everyone in the squad room turn back to what they were doing like they hadn't been hanging on every word he and his uncle exchanged. Even his partner, Ramón Herrera, took himself in the opposite direction with a short shake of his head and a wave of his hand.

Cursing under his breath in his mother's tongue, it took less than five minutes to empty his locker of street clothes and leave the station behind with a satisfying squeal of tires. By the time he drove his refurbished '64 Mustang convertible in the driveway of his new house and turned off the engine, Jake had ground his thoughts through his uncle's concerns three times.

Yes. The bust hadn't gone as planned. It still ended with no injuries and half a dozen SKL members in custody. Jake's only regret is that they hadn't captured Garza in the crack house. Lop off the head of the snake enough times, and the Dragons wouldn't be able to sustain their numbers. In principle. The problem is, another gang would simply take advantage of the weakness and slip into the open spot.

A problem for another day.

He stared through the windshield, mulling over the entire mess. Maybe the timing of this vacation wasn't such a bad thing. He didn't want to jeopardize his fellow officers, but he needed to lay his nightmares to rest. That wouldn't happen until Mateo Reyes got justice. Jake was convinced the Dragon's leader ordered his gangbangers to silence Mateo's older brother who'd taken exception to Garza "appropriating" his girlfriend. Julio Reyes snitched to the drug task force about a major drug buy and promptly disappeared — whether by design or through death, no one knew — while ten-year-old Mateo became collateral damage.

Maybe it was time to make a concerted effort to locate Julio. If he was alive, he might give the task force the means to shut down the gang permanently. If he wasn't, well, at least Jake would know he'd done everything in his power for Mateo.

Banishment from the station didn't have to be an issue. Jake could count on his partner, Ramón, to do some legwork for him. There were several other official connections he might tap. The trick was to stay off his superior's radar. When it came to his command, Captain Julian Munroe didn't make idle threats. Nephew or not, if he caught Jake digging into the Reyes case, he could kiss his career goodbye.

No way could he let that happen. He didn't miss his cheating ex-girlfriend, but he sure as hell would miss his job. He wasn't kidding when he said police work was his life. If he'd spared little time for the social niceties before Daniela kicked him to the curb, it had become nonexistent in the four months since they split.

Just the thought of playing civilian the next four weeks made his chest tighten. Putting his new home in order would take a few days, tops. He needed to build shelving for the cases of books stacked in the middle of his living room. He was barely functional in the kitchen, although he had set up his exercise room and new bedroom suite. He didn't have much in the way of furniture — Daniela had decorated their two-bedroom apartment to her taste so he hadn't fought to keep any of it—and he planned to take his time filling the rest of his new home.

That still left him with over three-and-a-half weeks to kill. A trip might be a great idea if there was someplace he wanted to go. Inactivity in another location, no matter how ideal, was as good as Chinese water torture to Jake. As for his uncle's other suggestion, find some drop-dead gorgeous woman to take the edge off?

With a snort, Jake climbed out of his car and walked toward his front door. Yeah, right! His job didn't exactly keep him knee-deep in nice women, and the last time he'd taken the edge off with a drop-dead gorgeous woman, he'd lost a friend to Daniela. And he wasn't thinking about the German Shepherd he'd picked up from the pound early in their relationship, although he did miss training Riker.

He shook the memories away. No. He'd spend the next few weeks trying to locate Mateo's older brother without his uncle looking over his—

Something's wrong.

The subliminal warning froze Jake's fingers in mid-turn on the front door key and flipped his numbed senses over to alert status. Abandoning the key in the lock, he scanned the immediate area. Four lone cars were parked on the street. All appeared empty, as were the neatly cut lawns trimmed by hedges and dotted with cottonwoods.

Jake frowned. At five o'clock in the morning, he expected little else. His research had led him to this older neighborhood in Riverton, an oasis of sedate family life tucked into charming Spanish bungalows near the South Platte River. After two weeks in his new home, he was willing to bet the only prowling done here was of the amorous tomcat variety.

An audible whisper of sound from behind the house dangerously rocked this belief.

Muscles drawn tight, he rejected the idea of calling for backup. Facing his uncle's ire again in less than an hour didn't appeal. He didn't dare walk near that lion's den again without a damned good reason.

Pocketing his key, his foot hit the first step off the porch. Quietly, he eased the gun from his side holster. With the familiar weapon gripped in his left palm, Jake moved to the corner of the bungalow. He darted a look around the stucco corner and sharpened his perceptions on the rush of adrenaline. A pre-dawn river fog swirled in the shadows between his house and the neighbor's, reducing visibility considerably. Not ideal conditions.

Taking two deep breaths, he dashed toward the solid, wood fence that separated him from the back yard. Crouched low, he moved through the gaping gate. "Halt! Police," he called, sure he saw movement several yards away.

He waited a couple of heartbeats to see if his command would be obeyed, then cursed. With no further movement, it was impossible to get a solid fix on his prey. Something, or someone, was there. But where was the bugger?

"Show yourself," he declared, all the while hoping he wasn't chasing shadows. Peering through the thinning haze, he bluffed. "I've got you in my sights."

An odd, strangled sound met the challenge. "Don't shoot! I-I'm coming out."

Jake released some of the air dammed in his chest,

one big question answered. That tremulous voice, though weak and barely heard, hadn't come from some prowling feline.

It wasn't that he minded appearing paranoid. After all, acute awareness of his surroundings had kept him alive through more than nine years of police work, not to mention the incident this morning that had earned him the dubious honor of a long vacation. But, for some reason, he found it hard to believe there was actually someone in his own backyard.

A silhouette detached from the shadows to his left. A shiver of apprehension slid up his spine. He'd swear the movement he'd first spotted was directly in front of him where the back gate bisected the hedge to the alley. "Are you alone?"

"No, sir." The owner of the voice stepped into the arc of watery light seeping from the front of the house. "I mean, yes, sir."

Mateo? Hard, merciless fingers clutched Jake's insides and gave a sickening twist. A prickling chill raised the hairs on the back of his neck. Either he'd fallen over the edge as his uncle suspected or he was looking at a ghost.

He shrugged off the stinging memory. He hadn't stalked a ghost, just a skinny, fresh-faced kid who looked like one. Jake eyed the pricey 35mm camera that hung around the boy's neck, numerous questions vying for expression. He chose the most pressing one. "Are you alone or aren't you?"

"I-I'm alone." The boy's bottom lip quivered before he bit down on it. A lone tear traced down one grimy cheek. "M-My friend got away."

Jake watched its mate slide down the opposite

cheek. Uh-oh. Tears. They did him in every time, especially the sincere I-can't-believe-I-did-it-either and I'm-real-sorry kind of tears. Disgust at his weakness roughened his voice. "What's your name, son?"

Frightened brown eyes fixed on his left hand. "E-Eric, sir."

The gun suddenly felt heavier. When exactly had he lost his momentum, when he called the boy "son" or when the kid called him "sir"? Most likely, it was the four month old regret ricocheting through his head like a stray bullet that did the most damage.

With a last scan of the empty yard, he lowered his arm to holster his weapon. "Okay, Eric," he said sternly. "First, we'll go into the house. You're going to tell me your life's story, right down to the part that explains what you're doing with that fancy camera under my hedge. Then, we'll decide what to do with you. Understood?"

Eric's head jerked up and down. He walked toward the front yard, his back poker stiff. He looked like a miniature soldier, bravely marching through the cold dawn to face the firing squad. No show of fear on the outside. Quaking like Jell-O on the inside.

Jake followed, trying not to let the kid get through to him. It didn't work. His last thought before he abandoned himself to the final softening process was of the firm, king-sized bed he'd been ready to fall into for the past two hours. "Hell of a way to start a vacation," he muttered.

Then he smiled wryly at the sound of his displeasure. It wasn't as if he'd been all that thrilled with the time off in the first place. At least he wasn't bored yet. What more could a man ask?

12

~~~

Carrie Padilla wished she could crawl back into bed. Maybe, under it. Any day that included a cop on her doorstep didn't promise to be a good one. A policeman appearing at the crack of dawn spelled disaster. There must be some mistake.

The hope prompted her to peek through the peephole a second time to examine the identification she'd demanded. Her heart racing, she sucked in one short, shaky breath of air. Then another, longer one. Her head spun with the effort, so she had to settle her forehead against the door.

She couldn't chance a one-on-one confrontation with a uniform again. Not this close. She may have beaten the impulse to fall apart every time a siren sounded in the distance or a police car appeared in her rearview mirror, but did she dare test herself with closer contact?

"If you'd like to call the station, Sergeant Grenich will vouch for me." The voice was deep, authoritative, impossible to ignore.

Opening the door wouldn't be her first choice. Then, neither would it be second or third. But Officer Jake Stefani wanted to speak with her and she didn't have an excuse for turning him away. At least, no valid excuse.

Her fingers fumbled with the safety chain as she glanced down at her sweaty exercise gear. Sports bra, covered by the sleeveless Colorado Rockies T-shirt her husband bought her before he died. Her old running shorts, a tad less loose thanks to her recent make-up-for-the-loneliness, chocolate-peanut butter ice cream splurges. Running shoes with low-cut athletic socks.

She wore less to the local swimming pool, so why

did she suddenly feel so naked? She was afraid it was due to more emotional reasons than physical ones. The problem was she didn't have the nerve to ask the man outside to wait until she was better able to cope. He wasn't likely to wait forever.

Unable to avoid the inevitable any longer, she threw open the door while one trembling hand tucked tendrils of damp, auburn hair back into her ponytail. Disconcerted to find herself nose to chest with the policeman, she stepped backward, her desire to bolt suddenly stronger. At only a few inches over five feet, she'd experienced her share of "tiny attacks" in the past, but never with this kind of intensity.

Amazingly enough, the uniform didn't cause the problem. The man behind it did. Although he couldn't quite lay claim to six feet, his crisp, dark blue shirt clung to a broad chest, his trousers molded to muscular legs. He didn't have the brawny physique of a body builder though, more the sleek, leashed power of a man trained in martial arts. Good heavens, but his biceps looked strong. Rock hard.

Something distinctly feminine within her quickened. Were arms like those capable of tenderness? A woman would feel safe there, secure, if she wasn't crushed to death first.

Chasing the unruly notion away, she gazed elsewhere. The dark shading of the man's square jaw suggested a beard needing two close shaves a day. His full lower lip was sensuous and bound to cause heartache, if a woman weren't tripped up first by the mischievous bump of a slightly crooked nose. She blinked when she reached the kindest, warmest brown eyes she'd ever seen. They were the same rich shade as

Swiss chocolate. Soft. Mouthwateringly tempting.

Wow. Too bad she was on a no-man diet.

She pushed away the troublesome rush of awareness and ruthlessly reminded herself she was ogling a cop. She urged her lungs to breathe. "What can I do for you, Officer?"

"Mrs. Padilla?"

Her insides vibrated to the sinfully deep rumble of his voice before she could clamp down on the new sensation. "I'm Carrie Padilla." *Please have the wrong woman!*

"Sorry to bother you at this hour, Mrs. Padilla, but we need to discuss your son."

"Eric?"

"Um. Hi, Mom."

Carrie's eyes widened. The boy who edged into sight from behind the officer's bulk couldn't possibly be *her* son. This boy appeared too small, too grimy, and he wore a familiar red windbreaker and an unfamiliar, guilty expression. She turned to stare up the flight of stairs behind her. Her heart sank. "Eric," she whispered, wondering when her son had sneaked from the house. She'd been up for several hours thanks to her recent bout of insomnia and Eric hadn't passed her bedroom door while she ran on the treadmill.

Looking back at the pair on her doorstep, she fought harder to marshal her wits. Her stomach flip-flopped unevenly when her gaze fixed on the uniformed figure at Eric's side, but she thrust her personal problems aside as motherly instincts kicked in. She'd confront the Devil, himself, to protect Eric. "What are you doing with my son?"

The cop frowned. "Could we come in, please?"

She had to fight her immediate impulse to deny this man access to her home to motion them inside. Closing the front door, she led the way to the living room. Eric sat at one end of her forest green sofa. Only after the policeman moved to the other end did Carrie perch on the wing chair positioned opposite, a move she regretted when she realized the man remained standing. She waved at him. "Please sit."

He hesitated, but then took a seat on the couch.

Somehow, she didn't feel any less overwhelmed looking him straight in the eye with only a mahogany coffee table between them. She ignored the peculiar feeling they'd drawn battle lines, with her on one side, her son and his escort on the other. She looked at Eric. "What did you—"

"Mrs. Padilla, before we begin, you might want to call your husband."

Her gaze jolted the length of the couch. "My husband is dead," she said. Six years should have dulled the ache of her loss, but she was dismayed to hear it blurted out loud. Who knew she'd need all her defenses in place before six a.m.?

"I'm sorry."

His sincerity appeared real, but she was unwilling to deal with the emotions compassion dredged up. She squared her shoulders. "Could you please tell me what's going on?"

"I found your son in my back yard." He glanced at Eric. "He was engaged in a potentially harmful activity I thought you should know about."

What in blazes is a *potentially harmful* activity? "What was he doing?"

"Preparing to vandalize my house."

"What?" She stared at Eric. "Is this true?"

Her son's eyes dimmed behind a flood of tears. His head bobbed up and down. His mouth opened, but no explanation came out. He simply fell apart. In seconds, her little boy was sobbing as if his heart would break.

Carrie scooted from her chair, rounded the coffee table, and knelt at his feet. She enfolded his trembling body in her arms and castigated herself for not registering how abnormally quiet that he'd been since he entered the house. He was in shock. The last thing he needed was her yelling at him.

"Shh, baby. It's all right. We'll work it out. It's okay." She pressed a gentle kiss against his temple. "Ah, honey, don't cry."

Jake couldn't decide which bothered him the most, the stricken look on Carrie Padilla's face or the hopeless sounds ripping from Eric's narrow chest. He'd always been a sucker for distressed females and kids, and these two served as a double-shot.

He couldn't shake the similarities between Mateo Reyes and Eric. Neither did it help that Eric's mom was one of the sexiest women he'd ever met. His tastes normally ran to tall, sultry brunettes, but there was something about this petite woman's girl-next-door look that was firing his libido big-time.

Her eyes, a delectable shade of caramel with flecks of amber, drew him in deeper every time he looked at her. What her curvaceous body did to the sports tee and running shorts combo she wore should be outlawed. Clinging, damp material and flushed skin was a deadly combination. As if that weren't enough, she had the most exquisite legs. The color of cream with a light splash of coffee. Smooth. Sexy. Nearly perfect.

His gaze dashed to her left ankle. The mole he'd noticed above her tennis shoe winked back at him, calling for his attention as a neon sign never could. It shouted, "Start here!" just like one of those connect-the-dot books he'd hoarded as a kid. He had a compulsive desire to follow the instruction, to nibble on that ankle and work slowly over the rest of her dewy skin to see if he could somehow develop a pattern.

Caught by the fantasy, his lips twitched. Who cared if there was a picture there? The seeking, all by itself, would make the trip worthwhile. In fact, his entire vacation might not be enough time to do justice to such an exploration.

Jake's jaw clenched against the unreasonable cascade of desire. Was he nuts? This woman's legs had nothing to do with his purpose here. And, if the impenetrable wall he'd watched form in her eyes a few minutes ago had meaning, he wouldn't get a chance to go exploring in any case.

He was dragged back to the situation at hand when Eric began to speak between his sobs. "I know it was dumb, Mom. Davy said. B-but I...we wanted to be in the club. We just want to be in the club!"

With one look at Carrie's bewildered expression, Jake knew the explanations would have to come from him. He leaned forward in a deceptively casual pose and shoved his libidinous thoughts back where they belonged. His objectivity was still intact inside him. Somewhere.

"The story I got was that Eric and Davy wanted to join a group at school. However, the kids wouldn't let them in unless they'd agree to be initiated. I'm afraid it's the initiation which got them into trouble."

18

"What did they do?"

"They were supposed to break some windows on a house and take pictures to prove they'd done it."

He wanted to believe the older kids had dreamed this one up knowing the boys wouldn't have the guts to do it. But, he'd been a cop too long. Gang recruiters got younger and bolder every day. It angered him to see them thriving on the vulnerability of naive kids like Eric. Like Mateo.

"I see."

In those two softly spoken words, Jake heard Carrie's emotional turmoil, her silent acceptance of what he'd left unsaid. He hated to be the one to bring harsh reality into this woman's safe, secure world. "They were only thinking about it," he assured her. "They didn't do it."

She clutched her son to her, as if that alone would protect him from harm. It astonished Jake how quickly his own tension lifted upon the sight of her relief.

Eric pulled away. "Are we going to jail now, sir?"

Jake had noticed the boy's respectful tone and manner earlier. Too often, when forced to deal with a youngster in the course of his work, he saw too little politeness and even less honest deference to authority. He didn't think the kid was on the road to ruin—yet—but there was no point in losing this opportunity to set the boy on the right path. "Well, kid, that's why we're here. You, your mother, and I have to work something out."

Carrie leaned back and frowned. "Eric, how did you get out of the house anyway?"

"The apple tree under my bedroom window."

"That tree is twenty years old and not nearly strong

enough!" She took a deep breath. "Never mind, we'll discuss that later. What I really want to know is why you'd consider such a stupid, dangerous stunt in the first place. And, where's Davy? Why isn't he with you?"

In that instant, Eric looked less anxious than disgusted. "Davy ran away. He saw him," her son nodded toward Jake, "before me. He didn't get that gun pointed at *him*. When I get to school..."

It took too long for his words to sink in. When they did, Carrie's heart nearly stopped. "Sweet mercy," she whispered, her gaze darting to the officer. "You shot at my son?"

The man shook his head and began to speak, but the only words she picked out had something to do with "procedure" and "self-defense." The rest was buried under the emotional maelstrom that flooded her head.

The last time a cop pointed a gun at someone you loved, he died.

She fought the nausea that clawed at her stomach and closed her eyes against the painful images seared into her brain six years ago. Flashing lights. Uniforms. Fear. The black rush of oblivion. Dear God, she couldn't do this again!

Chapter Two

Jake smothered a curse as he registered the pallor sweeping across Carrie's cheeks. Eric could have gone all day without mentioning the details of his capture. Jake's precautions were warranted. However, for the first time in his career, he felt compelled to defend his actions to a civilian. No longer sure Carrie was listening to his stumbling efforts to reassure her, he wound down. "I didn't know I was tracking a couple of small boys."

When she didn't respond, he frowned. "Car...uh, Mrs. Padilla? Are you all right?"

She blinked. "I'm grateful," she said softly, then cleared her throat, "you didn't shoot my son."

"I'm glad I didn't have cause." He couldn't decipher the disturbing shadows in her eyes. But the longer he sat there, the more conscious he became of the strange undercurrents in the room. There was more going on here than her alarm over the details of her son's brush with the law.

"For God's sake, Eric, what were you thinking?" She stared at her son. "Why would you do something so dangerously stupid?"

Fresh tears retraced the path down his grimy cheek. "I didn't mean, it wasn't supposed to—"

He flushed and stammered on. "I-I want to be big,

like the kids in the club. They do all kinds of stuff 'cause they're older, and I thought—"

Eric hiccupped and hung his head. "I messed up."

An understatement. Carrie shook her head to loosen the knots across the top of her shoulders. "Honey, you're eight years old. You don't need to grow up that fast."

The back of his hand swiped at the tears on his cheeks. "Do, too."

"Whatever for?"

"'Cause you need a man 'round the house."

"What?" She fought hard not to laugh at the incongruous statement, waiting for the punch line. One look at Eric's face told her there wasn't one. "You're kidding, right?"

He worried his lip with his teeth. "Davy says girls need a guy to take care of them. He says it's not—" His nose wrinkled in thought. "He says it's not natural, yeah, that's it." He smiled slightly, as if proud of his memory. "It isn't natural for girls to take care of things. I figure you don't have Dad to do it, so I have to."

Not knowing whether to be horrified, embarrassed, or amused by the unexpectedly mature notion, she darted a look to her right. She wasn't surprised to see masculine amusement warring with commiseration in the policeman's expression. Her cheeks heated.

"If I grow fast," Eric added, "I can get a job and take care of you. You won't have to work so much. I can quit school when I'm sixteen. Then you won't have to work at all." He beamed at her, his logic firmly planted in his mind.

At a loss, Carrie said nothing. When had her increased office hours begun to trouble Eric? Didn't he understand it was only temporary? She'd explained how important it was that she increase her sales performance. Their future, Eric's security, depended on it. She wouldn't fail him. Not ever.

Officer Stefani—she couldn't allow herself to think of him as Jake—jumped into her stunned silence. "Eric, who told you it was okay to quit school at sixteen?"

"Davy says—"

Carrie laid her hand on Eric's arm. "It seems to me Davy says entirely too much."

There was no question where the adult-sounding sentiments had originated. And, she vowed, as soon as she got to the office Davy's father, Sam O'Reilly was going to get a piece of her mind. It didn't matter the man was her best friend's husband or that he was Carrie's boss. He had no business putting these archaic notions in her son's head.

Was it any wonder Eric had been acting so unpredictably these past months? She'd suspected he was having difficulty at school, even questioned his teachers several times, but no one could identify any particular problems. If only she'd looked closer to home!

Eric patted the top of her hand like he was the adult and she, the child. "Mom, I'll be sixteen in only seven and a half more years. You'll be okay 'till then, won't you?"

She had to admire her son's motives—they were pure enough—even if his methods threatened to give her hives. "Honey, it's not your job to worry about me. Despite what Davy or his dad says, I'm perfectly capable of taking care of things. But, I promise," she held up three fingers, "Scout's honor, if I need any help, you'll be the first one I call. Okay?"

"Okay."

When her son gave her a wobbly smile, she was struck by the ridiculousness of the situation. Looking at the man sitting on the other end of her couch, she saw an expression that had to be similar to the one on her own face. For an instant, her barriers dropped. She couldn't quite pull herself from the depths of the man's caring eyes. The warmth of his understanding washed through her. A silent but tangible connection grew between them. Without reservation, she smiled her appreciation.

Jake stared at the promising softness of Carrie's lower lip and experienced an inexplicable urge to tell Eric he could stop worrying about his mother. That she now had someone to look after her. What man wouldn't relish the job of bringing happiness to her wary eyes, of putting a satisfied smile on her kissable mouth?

Whoa, buddy!

The wholly improper sentiments jolted him to his feet. Maybe his uncle was off base to force his vacation, but he was more tired than he'd thought to be having no-holds-barred daydreams about a woman he'd just met. It was all his uncle's talk about drop-dead gorgeous women and taking the edge off that was making him crazy. "You two have a lot to discuss before you have to get ready for work and school," he said. "I'll go now."

Carrie rose, too. "You aren't pressing charges?"

Jake straightened his hat over his brow. "No. I decided to bring Eric home and talk to you instead."

"Thank you," she said softly. "I'm sorry he caused so much trouble. I promise it will never happen again."

"I'm sure it won't," he replied, barely able to catch himself from testing her given name on his tongue. Only

24

a prized fool would handle this incident in such an unprofessional fashion, but he had to get out of this room, out of the house, or make an even bigger fool of himself.

"If it's okay with your mom," he said to Eric, "I'd like to see you this afternoon. When you get home from school, maybe you and Davy can come over so we can talk, get to know one another. We'll discuss this business of quitting school, among other things. Okay?"

Eyes wide, the kid nodded. Jake knew he had to be wondering how he'd gotten off so easily, but Jake couldn't possibly explain what he was feeling to an eight-year-old boy. He wasn't prepared to look too closely at it himself.

Turning back to Carrie, he searched his mental files for an appropriate form of retreat. "It was nice to meet you, Mrs. Padilla."

Before he could find a reason to linger, he strode from the room and out of the house. He didn't breathe until he was on the other side of the front door.

"Wait!"

The feminine voice stopped Jake only halfway to the street. He hesitated briefly with his back to Carrie then returned to the bottom of the porch steps. He ordered his face into a blank inquiry. "Did I forget something?"

Like my wits? My common sense? Or maybe my sanity?

"Uh, well," she said, her gaze dropping to the vicinity of his chest where his badge was pinned. When she looked into his eyes, she frowned. "I forgot to ask where you live. I need to know where to deliver Eric this afternoon." Her voice sounded loud and harsh in the thinning morning fog.

Jake registered the stiffness of her stance, the way

25

her right hand pressed against her breastbone like she felt the need to hold in some strong emotion. The distance between them was palpable, despite the fact that his semi-official visit was now behind them. He willed her to relax and pointed two doors down, across the street. "Right over there."

Carrie fidgeted on the top step. "The Seibert's house?"

"I bought it a few weeks ago." Imagine the luck of practically living next door to this woman. He smiled. "Looks like we're neighbors."

"Oh. Wonderful."

He felt his smile congeal on his face. It was wonderful, he agreed, but he got the feeling she meant the opposite. He couldn't discern anything out of the ordinary in either her even tone or neutral expression, but he'd missed something. Something important.

He frowned. *What did he say?*

~~~

"I can't believe I'm raising a near criminal." Joan O'Reilly splashed creamer into her sweetened coffee and stirred it with several haphazard motions. Then, she slumped over Carrie's Spanish-tiled kitchen counter to her original position of over-dramatized dejection.

Carrie didn't laugh because she knew her best friend tended to mask insecurities with theatrics. "Relax, Joan. You didn't send Davy off to prison." She carefully lifted the last hot cookie off the baking sheet she'd removed from the oven. "Besides, Eric's with him."

It was late afternoon. The boys had gone across the street after school more than an hour ago to make their apologies to her new neighbor. She wouldn't allow her mind to travel over there with them. Not before it became necessary anyway.

She spooned several tidy globs of cookie dough onto the empty baking sheet before she spoke again. "I still can't believe Davy told you about this morning on his own initiative."

"My son may now be a juvenile delinquent, but at least he's an honest one." Joan raked both hands through her red, pixie haircut. "I guess that's something anyway."

Carrie couldn't think of even one reassurance. Her confidence in her own parenting skills was severely dented right then, too. She'd been both mother and father to Eric since he was a toddler. But, her son seemed to have grown up too quickly in recent months. She'd begun to wonder if he might need a male figure—not a father, necessarily, but another role model—in his life, after all.

Like it or not, this morning's escapade answered that question. The trouble was what could she do about it? It wasn't as if she had a plethora of male role models running around the edges of her life. The few married men she knew had children of their own to raise. Joan's husband, Sam, was a good man and Carrie was grateful for his willingness to include Eric in father and son activities alongside Davy, but she didn't want her son growing up thinking she couldn't take care of them.

She'd spent the past few years successfully tossing every single man she met beyond arm's length, so to whom could she turn for advice? Inexplicably, the image of her undeniably masculine, attractive new neighbor popped unannounced into her brain. Unnerved by both its immediacy and clarity, she blinked away the picture. "Stop looking for trouble," she said, not sure who needed the suggestion more, Joan or herself. "The boys aren't going to jail, and they are sorry."

That perked up her friend. "I should hope so. Even if two weeks grounding doesn't do the trick, they aren't likely to forget how much it'll cost them to fix my broken camera. Working off the price of its repair will take care of chores through Halloween."

"With any luck," Carrie added, "they'll both be in college before they're that adventurous again."

Exchanging a glance, they grinned and shook their heads. "Nah!" they said in unison.

Carrie knew there was one constant, besides an extraordinarily strong bond, between their sons. What one didn't think of, the other did. Their relationship reminded her of her friendship with Joan. They'd been in each other's pockets since second grade, when Joan knocked down Frankie Bowen on the playground for teasing Carrie about her hand-me-down clothes and lack of "real" parents.

"Thank goodness, our boys' adventures don't usually run counter to the law." She shuddered to think about this morning's close call, but forced the memory away before it could run away with the peace of mind she'd worked to cultivate all day.

Joan sobered. "Is that why you're still so upset?"

"Who says I'm upset?"

"Carrie, that's the fourth unbaked cookie you've eaten in the past ten minutes." Joan wiggled four fingers on one hand in the air, as if to prove her count. "The way I figure it, at the rate that dough is disappearing you'll have to mix up another batch."

She examined the empty spoon in her hand, and then hid the evidence of her guilt by scooping up another chunk of dough. "What has that got to do with anything?"

"You're just like me." The fingers Joan used to point out her indiscretion dipped into the bowl. "We both pig out when we're stressed." Popping the fat raisin she unearthed into her mouth, she smacked her lips. "Mmm. Delicious. Exactly why did you say you were making these cookies?"

Carrie turned away to slide the baking sheet into the oven. She pressed the timer button, taking time to form a coherent answer. What could she say? It made more sense to bake cookies than to sell her house and run to her in-laws in Florida? It was almost as ludicrous as her idea to hang shutters over the front windows. Blocking the sight of her beloved sunshine and the bloom of plants, just to shut one man out of her life, was no solution either.

This alarm she was feeling was admittedly out of the ordinary, but she refused to allow it to be more than temporary. She'd recapture her equilibrium soon enough. If baking cookies would help her adjust to the idea of a cop practically living on her doorstep, she'd bake cookies. Maybe if she saw the man without his uniform, at home with a loving wife, maybe a couple of kids, she'd be able to pry his bedroom eyes from her head and forget the weird effect the mere thought of his smile seemed to have on her capacity to breathe.

Sweet mercy! Now she had the vision of the man without his uniform in her head!

"Yoo-hoo! Earth to Carrie."

"Huh?"

"I asked—"

Cheeks flaming, she yanked her naughty imagination into line. "Yeah, the cookies," she said aloud. "I already told you why I'm making them. Stefani could have dragged our boys off to the police station. He didn't. I have to thank him somehow." Considering how badly things could have gone this morning, cookies seemed inadequate. But she had to do something so she could crawl back into her life and forget today ever happened.

She sipped at her cold coffee and grimaced. "Besides, I always welcome new neighbors this way. You know that. I'm just killing two birds with one stone."

"Neighbors, as in plural? He's married?

Questioning her neighbor's marital status was another road Carrie didn't want to travel. "Of course, he's married. Why else would he buy a four bedroom house in a family-oriented neighborhood? I'll bet he has half a dozen kids."

Making the sexy Italian's babies would be no chore.

The errant thought startled her so badly she choked. Disguising it as a cough, she eyed her friend. "Anyway, why are you so interested? Don't tell me you've finally tired of your husband's Neanderthal views on women."

"Ouch." Joan's smile twisted at the familiar tease. "You couldn't let that one pass, could you? Sam doesn't mean half the things he says on that subject, you know." She shrugged sheepishly. "Okay, yeah, he's old-fashioned. He'll be a Marine until the day he dies, but his protectiveness is one of the things I love about him. He's also very proud of you since you passed the real estate exam and went to work for him. A real male chauvinist wouldn't care."

Carrie felt the rebuke. She loved Sam as much as she loved Joan. The trio had attended high school together and, even then, Sam was the burly jock protecting his girlfriend and her best friend. He'd looked after Carrie until Eric's dad, Tomás Padilla, came along their junior year. It was thanks to Sam that Carrie now had a job she enjoyed. He'd alternately pushed, bullied, and encouraged her through some hard emotional times after Tomás' death. It was Sam who'd framed her real estate license like the proud father she'd never really known.

"Carrie?"

She summoned a smile. "I know how special Sam is, Joan. However, our boys didn't dream up those ridiculous views on the necessities of wedded bliss all by themselves. I wish Sam would leave my love life alone."

"What love life?"

"Don't you start." She dumped her coffee dregs into the sink. "We have a deal."

"Uh, Carrie," Joan gestured towards the oven, "better grab those cookies."

"But, the timer—"

She glanced at the stove sensors and groaned. *How had the broiler turned on?*

Rushing across the kitchen, she yanked the oven door open only to have acrid smoke billow out and choke off her air. Waving wildly, she removed the cookie sheet and dropped it on the stovetop. Staring at the neat lines of charcoal lumps, moisture pricked at her eyes. "I should have eaten them all before I cooked them," she mumbled, bewildered by the urge to cry.

"Nothing's gone right today."

"Forget those. They're history." Joan tugged her away from the stove and pushed a plate of golden-hued cookies into her hands. "Take these over to your new neighbors and say hello. I'll take care of the last batch."

When Carrie didn't move, she gave her a little nudge in the right direction. "Go, Carrie. Stop cowering in your kitchen. You'll feel better when you get it over with."

Chapter Three

She was across the street before her step faltered. It occurred to her that she'd been perfectly content cowering in her kitchen. When she came home from the office and started baking, she hadn't thought about how the cookies would be carried across the street. Facing a policeman twice in one day had to be above and beyond the call of duty.

It wasn't as if she were properly dressed for a visit, either. Gnawing on her lower lip, she checked her yellow, Capri pants. They weren't really all that bad, she decided. It was the garishly painted parrots marching across the matching halter top that were questionable. Bold and casual might be her personal style of choice but not necessarily the best first impression to convey to a conservative policeman's wife.

She scowled when she visualized herself in a backless, cerise cocktail dress, a silver platter piled high with oatmeal cookies balanced on her hand. The image was more apt to appeal to a particular policeman than his wife. That's the last thing she wanted.

Just march over there and get it done.

Determined strides carried her to her destination, her ponytail swinging against her shoulder blades as she bypassed the front door without knocking. Eric's voice coming from the side of the house drew her around the corner where she stopped once more.

"Hi, Mom," Eric grunted when he spied her from his upside down position along the stucco wall that provided backyard privacy for all of the homes in the neighborhood. It looked remarkably like he'd been hung over a line to dry like a wet sack in a brisk wind.

"Eric, what are you doing?" Carrie glanced at Davy, whose position was even more twisted on the opposite wall. Both boys were filthy, and she could see a tear in Eric's good school shirt. Brother! Were girls this hard on clothes?

"We're fixing the gate," the boys exclaimed in unison.

"That's all? You're not in trouble again, are you?"

Davy flushed. "'Course not."

"Oh."

"I needed their help." An all-too-familiar voice broke in at the same time a large hand holding a screwdriver and a hammer came to rest on top of the wooden gate the boys were holding in place. Jake Stefani's head and upper torso rose behind it.

Suddenly confronted with nothing but bare skin, Carrie's heart began to pound. The man was naked! No, he's not, she assured herself desperately. How many men did carpentry in the buff?

You may be looking at your first, a gleeful voice resounded from the depths of her head. Her mouth was suddenly drier than the Gobi Desert, not a surprising effect considering the sharp rise in her internal temperature.

"Okay, boys, you can let go now. I think that's got it," he said. Eric and Davy dropped off the wall as the gate swung open so that Carrie's neighbor could step around it. He stopped directly in front of her.

She watched a rivulet of sweat run a meandering line from one tanned collar bone, over a mile-wide chest, through a mass of dark, curly hair that eventually disappeared behind the top edge of the pair of well-worn, boot-cut jeans. Thank goodness! The man did have clothes on, although what was there wasn't nearly enough.

Carrie sucked air into her lungs, the spill of fresh oxygen in her bloodstream making her giddy. A uniform didn't do the man one iota of justice. Had she honestly thought seeing him out of it would make her feel better? Her nerve endings were bouncing around like rubber balls on a kindergarten playground. Her new neighbor was pure, unadulterated male and terribly sexy. No...dangerous.

"Do you mind?"

"Mind?" Would she mind tracing her fingertips over male contours again if they looked like this man's? Was the sky blue? Heaven forbid, but Jake Stefani was serious trouble, with or without his uniform.

"I hope you don't mind that I didn't send the boys right back, but they offered to help fix the gate. If I'd known how long it would take, I would have had them call home before we started."

Carrie struggled to pull her gaze above the muscular chest in front of her. "No." Her head shook back and forth. "I don't mind, at all."

Fantasies certainly dissipated quickly under an eight-year-old boy's scrutiny. "Hey, Mom, those cookies for us?"

Cursing the heat scorching her insides, she grabbed

onto the stability of her maternal role. "No, you little monster," she said. "Not after the way you polished off the batch I made especially for the school bake sale last week."

She mentally appliquéd a paper doll cutout of a police uniform over her neighbor's attractions before looking at him. "These are for Officer —"

"Jake. Just Jake, to my friends."

The husky interruption shredded the ill-fitting image in her head, stroking pleasurably against her jittery nerves. She told herself she was twenty-nine. Her hormones were completely under control. But, when another shuddery breath became necessary, her honesty raised a white flag. Fine. She was a little out of practice. It had been years since a man had made her heart flutter, let alone take flight, like this.

"These are for Officer Stefani and his wife," she explained to her son. She couldn't allow herself to use a half-naked man's first name, especially as he was a married, half-naked man.

"Then I won't have to share."

Her head snapped up too fast. The jolt traveled all the way to the base of her spine. "Excuse me?" Those shutters over the windows were sounding better and better by the minute. The question is would they be locking this man out or her in?

Hot, dark eyes challenged her. Tempted her. "I didn't mean I wouldn't share. I meant I can't share with my wife. I don't have one."

"Oh."

The blood roared in Jake's ears. Had he imagined the distance in Carrie's eyes earlier that morning? There was nothing reserved about the way she stared at him now, like he was a forbidden dessert in a bakery window on which she yearned to blow her entire diet. His mind was already running along similar paths he didn't dare follow in the presence of two innocent children.

He made the mistake of searching for that wickedly winking mole on her bare ankle. *Start here!*

"Maybe you'd better let me have the cookies before they end up in the grass," he suggested.

Carrie thrust the plate at him. "Of course."

"Thanks. They look good." Given a choice, he'd rather nibble on her.

He sniffed at the spicy aroma to smother the impulses tearing at his senses. "Mmm. My favorite, oatmeal raisin," he said, silently offering the plate to the boys.

"Me, too," they both cried, each taking a handful of cookies.

He offered the half-empty plate to Carrie. "Better grab one before they're all gone."

"No, thanks," she said. "I have this terrible habit of licking the bowl when I bake. My calorie level is already sky high." She made a face. "I'll have to do more exercises than normal tomorrow to work them off."

Yards of skin. Damp cotton clinging to full breasts. An enticing tangle of thick, cinnamon-colored hair. Jake couldn't think about it without also thinking of sumptuous desserts and binges of pleasure. "Um, it looks like these cookies are all ours, guys," he said heartily to block fantasies which could quickly become addictive.

Eric and Davy cheered his announcement.

Jake wondered if Carrie had caught the gist of his

wicked thoughts because her hand lifted to her chest as she backed up a step. His mental curse was sharp, succinct. He hadn't meant to make her retreat, literally and figuratively, behind that wall of hers again.

"I just wanted to thank you for what you did this morning. I mean what you didn't do."

He didn't know if she was referring to his not pressing charges or not shooting her son, but he hadn't forgotten her expression when she learned how Eric was captured. "I'm just glad I caught the boys," he shot a look at the two guilt-ridden culprits, "before they could do permanent damage to my windows or their futures."

The reminder of what was barely averted this morning overshadowed his mood. What he'd finessed out of the boys in the past hour about the group they wanted to join hadn't reassured him. If it *was* a gang and the kids had completed the initiation rite, he hated to think about the consequences. A talk with their school officer had hit the top of his "To Do" list.

As if she'd read his thoughts, Carrie frowned. "Well, anyway, thanks for bringing Eric home." She fidgeted, then blurted, "I have to go. I mean, I have a few more things to do before dinner is ready."

It took her son to stop her retreat. "Wait, Mom," he said. "What are you making?"

"I haven't decided." She shrugged. "I wanted to take you out for a celebration dinner, but I can't now."

"Why not?"

"Honey, as much as I'd like to pretend this morning never happened, I can't. Did you forget you're grounded?"

Eric's scuffed sneaker dug at a dandelion in the path that led from Jake's backyard.

He watched the kid wrestle with disappointment, looking so much like Mateo had the last time Jake had seen him. Hurt, confused, and so damned vulnerable. The temptation to avert a repeat of history, to wipe Eric's dejection away, was overwhelming. But there were some paths a person had to choose alone or it wasn't an effective decision. He held his breath until Eric spoke.

"Yeah, I forgot," he said to his mother. "I owe you two weeks and a clean garage." His smile was tentative. "Can we celebrate then?"

"You bet. It's a date."

Jake was intrigued by the relationship between mother and son. There was a steady link between them, a connection that excluded everyone around them. For some reason, he didn't like being on the outside of that circle. "What are you celebrating?"

Carrie's sunny smile nearly blinded him. "I'm an agent with O'Reilly Realty. I closed on a house today."

"That is something to celebrate," he congratulated. "Why don't I take you out to dinner? Friday night?"

No matter how surprised he was to hear himself ask for a date, it was nothing next to the confusion he read in her expression. "Oh, no, I can't!"

Suddenly, he wanted her acceptance like he hadn't wanted anything in ages. It would be easy to say he was only ensuring he'd be able to talk to her privately about Eric. The truth was his desire to date this woman had little to do with her son. He hadn't looked at another woman in months. He didn't have to understand where all this unusual chemistry was coming from to know he couldn't let it pass without exploring it. "Why not? You aren't grounded, too, are you?"

Carrie hesitated to answer, afraid of what might

come out of her mouth. There were too many odd thoughts, too many wild emotions, zipping through her mind. She couldn't go out with any man, let alone this one. She didn't dare. Her knees already felt like they were filled with unset tapioca pudding. The tantalizing smile tugging at Jake's sensual lips pulled her off balance. She couldn't think.

Why didn't he put on a shirt already?

"Just because you grounded Eric doesn't mean you can't go out, does it?"

"Of course not." She couldn't go because Jake was a man, he was a cop, and she wanted nothing to do with either.

"Then let me take you out to dinner so you can celebrate properly."

"Go on, Mom," Eric piped up. He stuffed a whole cookie into his mouth and mumbled the rest. "You never go anywhere. I can stay at Davy's Friday night."

Carrie watched to make sure he didn't choke on his mouthful. The instant he swallowed, she'd strangle him. How could he say such a thing? Just last week, she'd gone to that Chamber of Commerce thing with Sam and Joan. The week before that, there was that two-day seminar in Vail she'd attended with fellow real estate agent, Gary Smith.

So what if Gary was a co-worker and he'd brought his wife with him? The three of them had a great time together. Carrie was far from the social wallflower Eric suggested. It wasn't as if she wanted a real date or anything.

But—

Her thoughts veered off in a curious direction. Maybe she should accept this one. Just this once. If she

40

could actually make herself go out with Jake, she might be able to put more of the past behind her. She was tired of waiting for the memories to sweep over her unexpectedly whenever her guard came down. Besides, she did need something from Jake. Oddly enough, he was in a unique position to help her with her son.

Part of her screamed this man didn't have the answers she needed. He wasn't a nasty shot she could take to make her forget, an immunization against a painful past, and he was the last person to ask for guidance with Eric. She'd lost one loved one to the police. She couldn't lose another.

But another, quieter part of her was still in operation. "Dinner, Friday night," she said. "Sounds nice."

~~~

Carrie swept into her kitchen minutes later and, deliberately ignoring Joan's lifted eyebrow, strode over to the sink. Squirting too much dishwashing liquid into it, she scowled at the bubbles that grew rapidly beneath the gush of hot tap water. Her life was like that, she decided. One little squeeze too much and life bubbled out of control.

"How did it go?"

She dumped dirty dishes into the sink. "How did what go?" She scrubbed at a spatula.

"What's she like?"

"Who?"

There was a loud, rude sound behind her. "Stefani's wife! I hope she's not as bad as that Seibert woman. A walking dessert cart, that one, and not too particular who nibbled in her direction. Thank goodness, the Seiberts only lived in that house a year. Her husband's transfer was the best thing to happen to this neighborhood." Joan stopped to take a breath. "Please, please, please! Tell me Stefani's wife is normal...like us."

Carrie rinsed the spatula and dug a bowl out of the bubbles. She scrubbed and scrubbed until foam burgeoned to monumental proportions over her hands. "I wouldn't know if she's normal or not. He's not married."

A hush descended over the kitchen until Joan broke in with her usual finesse. "What's wrong, Carrie?"

She dropped the bowl back into the soapy water with a splash and whirled around. Water and bubbles drew an arc across the floor. "Wrong? How could anything be wrong? Life's great! It couldn't be better!"

Her friend handed her a dishtowel. "And that's why you're scouring those poor defenseless sunflowers off that bowl instead of putting it in the dishwasher like any other sane woman."

Carrie collapsed onto a stool and forced down an edge of hysteria. "I've really blown it this time, Joan."

"What did you do? Whatever it is, it can't really be as bad as you're making it out to be."

"It's worse." Her eyes stung. "How could I be so stupid? I said I'd go out with him."

"You weren't even gone fifteen minutes." Joan stared at her then laughed with delight. "You got a date between here and there? That's great. With who? Or is it 'whom'?"

Her head tilted thoughtfully as she studied Carrie. "Never mind. At this point, if it means you're going out with a man, even Frankenstein is acceptable. You may borrow my six-inch platform shoes. That ought to bring you up past his belly button."

Her agitation was unreasonable, but it didn't change the fact she couldn't cope with Joan's irrepressible razzing when her defenses were so seriously depleted. "Oh, right. Go ahead and laugh. I do something truly stupid, and you make jokes about my height."

"Sorry." Her gamine grin didn't look very penitent. "So, who's the lucky guy?"

"Jake Stefani."

Both of Joan's eyebrows rose, along with her voice. "You can't be serious."

She rose from the stool to pace the kitchen. "I'm not laughing, am I?"

"Ah, Carrie, what am I going to do with you? For more than five years, Sam and I have badgered you to start dating again." Joan poked a finger at her. "You've turned down Kitty Lawrence's hunky brother-in-law every time he's asked you out in the past three years, and you suddenly pick a cop? Why? Is it some kind of morbid fascination or something?"

Uncomfortable with the direction of the conversation, Carrie grabbed at the diversion. "Charlie Lawrence might look like that really hot James Bond actor, whatever his name is. He might make tons of money as an airline pilot," she argued, "but I'm still not interested in a relationship with the guy."

"You're interested in a relationship with Stefani."

"No! I didn't say that. I'm—"

Her pacing stopped abruptly. "For crying out loud, Joan, I don't want a relationship with *anyone*. If you'd been left alone as many times as I have, you wouldn't be all that eager to stick your neck out again either." She hadn't learned her lesson in childhood, but losing

43

Tomás was the final straw. Never again would she place her heart in jeopardy.

A lingering sigh escaped her. "Look, it just happened, okay? The man asked. I answered. Just like that, I made a date."

"But what were you thinking?"

Her brain was a bit fuzzy at this point. If the truth were told, she'd been in a daze since the crack of dawn when she discovered her miscreant son and a hot cop on her doorstep. She'd suffered more emotional extremes in the last ten hours than she'd allowed herself in years.

Joan grasped her upper arms. "Is it because of *what* he is, Carrie? Because if that's the sole reason, I think you've gone totally nuts." She gave her a little shake. "You don't even know if Stefani's one of them."

She didn't have to explain whom she meant because Carrie already knew who "them" were. In fact, she couldn't say the idea hadn't already been hovering at the back of her consciousness without her being aware of it. Still, she wasn't prepared for Joan's final shot.

"How can you think of dating this man when you won't even talk about what happened that day, let alone say the name of the policeman who killed your husband?"

Chapter Four

The question still haunted Carrie three days later. It was true. She didn't readily talk about the awful events of six years ago. Neither did she discuss the outcome of the police department's lengthy investigation. She was too scared of dragging the nightmare that ended her life with Tomás out into the open.

That wasn't a crime, was it? She knew the name of the policeman, the S.W.A.T. officer, who'd shot her husband. She'd seen his picture. That man wasn't Jake.

It didn't mean he wasn't there, too, among the horde of faceless uniforms in her memory. It's where her dilemma bogged down. If Jake was at the bank that fateful day, was he any less responsible than the man who'd actually pulled the trigger? Did she want to know for sure? After all, she did have to live next to Jake and, in this case, maybe ignorance *was* bliss.

Carrie rested her throbbing temple against the cool post on her brass bed. Her stomach churned. Considering her state of mind, tonight's dinner was more than ill advised, it was insane; and, she suspected, it wasn't just because of the uniform with which Jake covered his all-too-appealing body every day. She simply couldn't risk letting anyone get too close. One way or another, she'd lost too much of her heart already.

She was holding on to what was left.

Not that there was the slightest danger of losing her head over Jake, no matter what her deprived hormones might say to the contrary. It just made good sense to maintain a proper distance. It made better sense to avoid the possibility of temptation altogether.

She reached for the phone on the bedside table before she reminded herself why she'd accepted the date in the first place. She couldn't ignore the point of Eric's actions on Tuesday. It was imperative she arm herself against the forces which threatened her only child. She knew nothing about gangs or how to protect her son from them. She'd considered making an appointment with the policeman stationed at Eric's school, but couldn't quite bring herself to speak to a complete stranger. It was going to be tough enough to discuss her concerns with Jake.

The dichotomy of the situation wasn't lost on her. To go out with her neighbor, she had to forget what he did for a living. But what he did was the purpose of the date. "So, get over it," she muttered. "Get dressed, eat dinner, and make conversation. How hard can it be?"

Rummaging through her walk-in closet, one outfit after another hit the center of her bed. Finally, she gave up, flopped back on the pile, and mentally sorted the clothing smashed beneath her.

"Mom," Eric called from the open doorway, "you said you'd walk me to Davy's. Aren't you ready yet?"

Carrie laid an arm across her eyes. "I'm not going."

"What's wrong?"

"I have nothing to wear, that's what's wrong."

He had the temerity to laugh. "You've got tons of stuff to wear. Just pick something."

What did he think she was trying to do? There was nothing for a date that wasn't a date that wasn't a business deal. "If you can do better, go for it."

A variety of noises drifted from her decimated closet. "Hey, cool," Eric cried several minutes later, his voice muffled. "I never saw this before."

Curious about what she might have missed, Carrie sat up. Her eyesight blurred when she saw the red wine-colored swathe of silk Eric held up. Fashioned into an alluring one-piece jumpsuit, the bodice was held in place by two thin straps, depending on her breasts to provide for slippage. The peek-a-boo waistline, defined by ties on each side, created the illusion that one tug would bare more than a little flesh. The ankles were drawn together with two more ties.

She knew what it did for her figure, not to mention her self-confidence, although she'd never worn it after its purchase. It was her anniversary outfit, the one never celebrated because of Tomás' untimely death. She'd thrown it to the back of the closet and put it from her mind.

"I—" A huge ball in her throat blocked the words.

"C'mon, Mom," Eric wailed plaintively. "It's pretty. I bet Jake likes it, too." He waved the hanger and declared with more force, "Mooom, I like it."

Carrie weakened, but not, she told herself, because it was pretty or because Jake might like it. Eric was eager to get to Davy's house. Joan had fixed his favorite beef stroganoff dinner. It didn't matter what Carrie wore anyway, and she did need a morale booster.

Defeated, she rose from the bed to take the hanger from him. "Fine, Eric. I'll wear it." She checked her watch and gasped. "I'll call Joan to see if she can pick

47

you up."

Eric dashed for the door. "I'll get my stuff and wait downstairs."

Carrie smiled weakly at his departing back before dialing Joan's number to make her request. Then she removed her robe and, wearing only sheer panties and a strapless bra, slipped into the jumpsuit. All thumbs, she couldn't manage the intricate French braid she'd planned, merely brushing her hair away from her face. A dash of makeup, a spritz of her favorite carnation perfume, and she was ready.

Gathering up her purse and a light jacket, she sat down on the bed with a jerk. She wanted to burrow under the covers and never come out. Anxiety warred with...was it expectation? She identified the unusual emotions for what they were and moaned with frustration. This promised to be a very long night.

~~~

Jake hovered on Carrie's doorstep five minutes early, unable to settle down, unwilling to knock until he did. He was anticipating this night with entirely too much energy. In the short distance he'd walked from his car to her front door, his blood began to race, his hands grew sweaty. He hadn't felt this nervous about a date since Alicia Cope, the most popular cheerleader at his Colorado Springs high school, agreed to go to the junior prom with him.

The difference between then and now is he was looking for more than a chaste kiss behind the school gym from Carrie Padilla. He wanted, well, he wanted a lot more from his new neighbor than was appropriate on a short acquaintance.

What the hell was the matter with him? He'd been

fantasizing about Carrie since that first morning when it occurred to him to put a satisfied smile on her lips. He'd spent the past three days wondering how she'd look lying in his bed beneath him, her captivating caramel eyes blurred by desire, her lips pursed, begging to be kissed. Was she a soft, gentle lover, or passionate and aggressive? He was becoming obsessed with the answer.

His hiatus from work was partially to blame, of course. It wasn't as if he'd been left with much else to keep him occupied. After a full day's sleep, he'd talked to his partner about his plan to locate Julio Reyes. Ramón warned him to back off for a week to let things die down at the station. His uncle had made it clear he was watching his fellow officers, that anyone caught talking to Jake about work before his return were flirting with repercussions.

Much as he chafed at the delay, Jake agreed to wait. However, if the last forty-eight hours were any indication, he didn't stand a chance of surviving his downtime if he didn't find something to occupy him. There was a reason he'd resisted taking a vacation the past two years. The older he got, the less time it took for his restlessness to take over. The prospect of fidgeting through another twenty-seven days like a caged animal had him literally tearing at the walls.

He scowled at the thought of the guest bedroom he'd begun stripping of wallpaper when the door abruptly opened and halted his musing.

Eric beamed at him. "Hi."

"Hi, yourself." Jake hoped the boy hadn't been watching him stand on the doorstep gathering his nerve like a rookie on his first bust. "I didn't expect to see you

49

here. Weren't you going to Davy's?"

The door opened wider. "Davy's mom is picking me up." He pointed at a silver SUV pulling up behind Jake's car. "There she is. I'm outta here." He turned on his heel to pick up an overflowing backpack lying at the bottom of the stairs. "'Bye, Mom," he called before flying out the door.

"See ya, Jake," he said over his shoulder. "Mom'll be down in a sec. I got her something to wear so she should be almost ready." With that breathless salvo, he was gone.

Jake watched him climb into the SUV before he shut the front door. Then, he heard footsteps approach from overhead.

"Eric?" Carrie halted at the top of the stairs when she spotted Jake. "Oh. I didn't know you were here. Eric's gone?"

"He yelled that he was leaving, but I guess you didn't hear him." That response left him spontaneously, but now his capacity for speech dwindled away as he stared up the stairs.

Eric was responsible for this? For one not even nine yet, the boy had incredible taste. From the top of her auburn head to the cotton candy, pink toenails peeking from her high-heeled sandals, Carrie was walking temptation. Her hair fell from two gold combs in glossy waves over her exposed shoulders, an invitation to exploring fingers. Tiny gold studs in her ears complemented the dainty necklace at her throat and drew awareness to pulse points and sweet, tender skin.

His gaze slid over the sensuous material clinging to her curves. He envied the points where the silky stuff made contact with smooth, naked flesh. He skimmed over ties that promised more than a red-blooded man had a right to expect, and glanced at her covered ankle. *Start here!*

"I'll have to fight them off with a nightstick," he breathed huskily.

"Who?"

"Every conscious male at the restaurant." Beginning with him.

"Oh." Carrie suddenly wished the outfit was fashioned from armor plate instead of silk. It had given her sexual and emotional confidence when she'd originally bought it. But this was Jake and the bold, masculine appreciation in his intent gaze was unnerving. The black jeans, pale blue cotton shirt, and black leather moto jacket he wore added to the hot and dangerous look that melted her insides. She didn't know what alarmed her most, the weakness creeping into her bones or the fire raging out of control under her skin.

Suddenly, she wasn't so certain she could do this, even for Eric.

Swallowing the obstruction in her throat, she forced her knees to unlock and started down the stairs. Carefully. She refused to disgrace herself by falling directly into Jake's arms. "I hope this is all right. You didn't say where we were going, so I wasn't sure."

"It's perfect."

An awkward silence fell between them. Carrie wondered how she'd get through the hours ahead if her body continued to sabotage everything her mind told it. Never before had she felt quite this muddled.

"Would you like a drink before we go?" She needed something. Preferably, something numbing.

He shook his head. "We can have a glass of wine at

the restaurant, if you'd like."

A few minutes later, Jake had her comfortably seated on the passenger side of a beautifully reconditioned, red Mustang convertible. She didn't know much about muscle cars, but she knew someone had done a lot of work on this one. It looked like it had just rolled off a '60s assembly line.

She smoothed her fingers over the red-and-white leather seat enjoying its supple texture. Glancing across the interior, she found Jake watching her. "This is beautiful. Did you do all of this work yourself?"

"No. This was my dad's project." With a glance around the interior, his expression softened under what were clearly good memories. "I helped him whenever I could break away from my friends in high school. After I finished the academy, he gave it to me as a graduation gift. He died a short time later so I always feel he's still with me when I drive it."

Her pulse hitched at the reminder of his profession. "He must have been so proud of you."

Jake nodded. "He was pleased I followed in his footsteps."

His large hand came up and gently pushed her hair over her right shoulder, and she inexplicably lost the thread of conversation. Flames swept her skin from her neck to her breasts, downward to scorch the butterflies in her stomach. Her air froze in her lungs when his gaze settled on her mouth. Her lips began to tingle.

Sweet mercy! Was he going to lean across the center console and kiss her? She wet her lips in anticipation.

He cleared his throat. "I think I'd better leave the top up so we don't mess up your pretty hair," he said, turning away to fasten his seatbelt like he hadn't just felt the same soul-deep need to kiss her the way she wanted to kiss him. "Is there a particular place you like, or should I choose?"

Her impulse to leap out of the car and run back inside where she felt safe from her dangerously rebelling hormones sounded like a better plan. She clicked her seatbelt into place. "Anywhere is fine."

Jake devoted only a portion of his attention to his driving while he tried to come up with a topic of conversation to ease the tension he'd inadvertently built in the car the instant he touched Carrie. His mind was disgustingly blank. So much for all those communications seminars he'd taken over the years. Not one of them recommended kissing a woman senseless in front of her house.

The intimacy of the car was proving a liability. From where he sat, he had a particularly good view of the curve of Carrie's full breasts above the fabric of that silky thing she wore. Every time he looked at her, his chest tightened. All of his air got locked somewhere deep in his chest, and his brains seized up from the lack of oxygen.

When he nearly scraped the paint off a parked car, he brought himself up sharply and fixed his mind on the road. As much as he hated to admit it, he'd seen enough wariness in Carrie's eyes when she walked down her stairs to realize she had her defenses locked and loaded. His baser instincts would just have to be put on hold until the signals changed more favorably in his direction. He'd get a table between them. Maybe then he'd be able to talk without embarrassing himself.

~~~

Jake didn't break the silence again until they were

seated at an intimate table at one of his favorite surf-and-turf restaurants, screened on three sides by potted plants, their orders given to an attentive waiter. "So," he said, leaning forward, "tell me about this house sale we're celebrating."

Despite a couple of false starts, Carrie began talking. The hesitations between sentences got shorter and shorter until she was talking easily about the difficulties she'd had getting her clients into a house.

Jake studied her flushed skin when she ran down. "A year is a long time to work with one couple," he commented. "That's not the norm, is it?"

"It happens, but not often, thank goodness." She smiled. "I didn't mind sticking with the Anderson's though."

"Friends?"

"No, they were just special." Carrie sat back. "They couldn't afford much, and I think they just dreamed of owning a house when we first met. But there was something about them and their little girls. I couldn't resist making their dream come true.

"And it was worth every minute, Jake. You should have seen their faces when I handed them the keys to their new home."

There was no need to see her clients' faces. He could see Carrie's. It was obvious she loved her work. She sold homes and dreams, not houses. Jake admired the depth of her feelings, the intensity of her commitment. He wondered if she applied that same enthusiasm to everything, to everyone, she cared about. He suspected she had more passion than she knew what to do with and it spilled over into her work. The idea of redirecting all of that energy his way was tantalizing.

Lifting his glass, he toasted her success. "Here's to the Andersons' new home and hard working real estate agents who make the difference. I wish I'd had you when I was looking for my place."

Carrie sipped her wine before setting it down. "This may be an intrusive question, but why did you buy the Seibert house? It's rather large for a single person and not exactly in the mainstream. There are a lot of nice townhouses in Riverton."

"A townhouse or apartment wasn't big enough."

"Why not?"

He shifted uncomfortably in his chair. Discussing his relationship with Daniela wasn't his first choice to keep Carrie talking on a more intimate level. It had been a monumental mistake to allow sex and his mother's matchmaking schemes to push him into settling for less than what he wanted from a relationship. He and Daniela might have burned hot and heavy when Mama introduced them, but he'd learned the hard way he wanted gratification outside of the bedroom, as well as within. A partnership. *Fidelity.*

The thought of past mistakes cleared his mind as nothing else had so far. "I wanted a house," he explained. "I was in a relationship and considering a move to something bigger when I started looking."

"What happened?"

He shrugged. "My position on the force didn't suit Daniela."

It rankled he hadn't registered her preoccupation with his career mobility before moving in with her. They'd been having problems for some time, but he'd thought it was due to his erratic schedule and her claim they needed to spend more time together.

He almost felt sorry for the poor sucker she'd hooked up with...almost. Jake's initial anger when he learned his ex-friend and co-worker, Colin Hertz, was moving to Kansas City with Daniela in tow had burned out quickly. Those extra chevrons on Colin's sleeve weren't going to keep her in check if someone better came along.

Jake understood her insatiable need for things—she'd grown up without much and she was over-compensating—but thankfully, it wasn't his problem anymore. He'd vowed, then and there, his uniform would never come between him and a woman again.

Carrie's heart ached for Jake. He might appear nonchalant, but she suspected his ex-girlfriend's desertion had hurt him. The danger inherent in his work wouldn't be easy for any woman to handle, but to leave because of his rank was incomprehensible.

The woman was a fool.

The thought didn't bear up under scrutiny. "You still bought a house," she said.

"I'll need it eventually."

"I don't understand."

He smiled. "I don't intend to spend the rest of my life alone." He took her fingers in his palm. "Everything worked out for the best. Daniela and I didn't have what was necessary to make a life together, but I did find the house I wanted."

"Do you still love her?" Aghast the question tripped off her tongue, Carrie was too slow in removing her hand from his grasp.

His fingers threaded through hers and trapped her. One thumb stroked the top of her knuckles. His expression grew pensive. "This will probably make me sound like a jerk, but I'm not sure I ever did.

"I think it was the idea of marriage that appealed to me. Having grown up in a predominately Italian neighborhood, surrounded by huge families, I'd always expected to have one of my own someday." He shook his head. "I have a much better idea of what I want now."

Carrie hadn't intended to stir up so many uncomfortable memories. But now it was time to get away from personal issues. His love life was truly none of her business and, heaven knows, there was little about hers she wished to explore. Besides, they'd skirted a little too close to the issue of his work and she suddenly wasn't sure she wanted to delve into it far enough to address Eric's problems. Not tonight, at any rate. Jake, the man, was so much more appealing than, Jake, the cop.

She retrieved her hand to her side of the table. "I'm glad you found your home, Jake," she said. Selecting a hard roll from the basket between them, she was grateful when he went on to other, more innocuous, subjects.

Their meals arrived soon thereafter. Carrie watched Jake cut into his rare steak before she turned to her own meal.

If there was one thing she loved, it was sampling exotic, new foods. She didn't taste. She experienced. Upon the waiter's recommendation, she'd ordered one of the restaurant's specialties, stuffed calamari. The squid was aromatic and stuffed with rice, raisins and pistachio nuts. The chef had smothered it all in an appetizing sauce of tomatoes and wine. The first bite told her it was every bit as tasty as it smelled.

"This is fantastic," she enthused after a second bite. She allowed the combination of flavors to explode on her tongue before swallowing, closing her eyes to savor the savory aftertaste.

Jake was watching her when her eyes reopened.

"You've got to try some of this." Without thinking, she pushed her fork into another portion bursting with stuffing and leaned across the table to him.

The inexplicable expression that crossed his face as he obliged and placed his lips around her offering flustered her beyond belief. A bold glint filled his hot, dark eyes. His lips tugged on the fork. Carrie's fingers slipped on the handle, but she didn't drop it, her gaze drawn to his lips.

Jake leisurely chewed the seafood she'd fed him, the movement of his mouth blatant. Masculine. Arousing.

She was afraid to look down, afraid to discover herself melting into her seat as boneless as the cuttlefish on her plate. If Jake had touched her with a long, heated caress, he couldn't have made her any hotter. He was enjoying a lot more than the morsel in his mouth, and she knew it.

"That is good. Want to try some of mine now?" His husky tone stroked her senses and she almost moaned with pleasure.

"No! No, thank you," she stammered. "I know what steak tastes like." Why had the hostess placed them in such a stuffy corner? Would it be rude to run to the powder room? A dash of cold water sounded like heaven.

~~~

Despite Carrie's brief swell of alarm, the rest of the meal progressed without incident. In fact, by the time they'd finished dinner, she and Jake were conversing easily and she felt unreasonably mellow. Contented. It would be so simple to blame the glass of wine she'd consumed, but the facts were her new neighbor was entertaining and she'd enjoyed his company tremendously.

When Jake escorted her back to the car after dinner, he suggested a drive into the foothills above Boulder to watch the sun set over the sprawling metro area. She quickly agreed. She wasn't ready for their evening to end.

The drive to the base of Flagstaff Mountain took thirty minutes. It passed quickly, though, while they talked about Jake's plans to strip his house of the Seibert's modern styling and recapture its original Spanish roots. Once they hit the road winding up the mountain, Carrie caught glimpses of chipmunks scurrying among the rocks. A hawk circled for prey. She even spotted a couple of deer nibbling tender grass in the shelter of the pines. By the time they reached the first scenic turnoff the sun was setting, the puffy clouds to the east catching fire.

Jake pulled off the road. "Let's stop here. If we drive the last two miles to the summit, we'll miss the sunset."

Carrie agreed.

After locking the car, Jake walked with her to the small lookout where a dozen people had gathered. Breathing in the rich scent of evergreens and wild flowers she watched the clouds turn bright red, laced with pink and orange, against a sea of blue. The colors finally deepened to purple as the last threads of sunlight were swallowed by the mountain behind them. Street lights began to fill the darkness below.

Jake pointed at the collection of broad clay roofs that delineated the University of Colorado campus. She followed his finger as it traced the lights eastward over a number of communities that were often lumped together as metro-Denver. Car lights traced two straight lines along Hwy. 36 and Baseline Road, also known as the 40th Parallel, both major thoroughfares from Boulder eastward.

A cooler breeze swept down the mountain and cut through the light material of Carrie's pantsuit. Chilled, she put on her jacket and worked her hands into opposite ends of the cuffs. Jake placed his bulk along her back. "Lean into me," he suggested. "You'll be warmer."

She hesitated, but saw the wisdom of accepting his protection. Carefully relaxing into his broad chest, she rested her arms on his when they spanned her waist. "Mmm," she said, nestling further into his welcome heat. "It's been ages since I've taken the time to come here and see the city at night like this. Thanks for suggesting it."

"You're welcome," he said over her head. His arms tightened briefly. "Still cold?"

When she shook her head, her hair briefly snagged on the zipper of his leather jacket. Carrie hadn't felt this snug and secure in years, and it had more to do with the man who held her than the protection he provided against the breeze. "Not any more, thank you. I'm nice and toasty."

Jake crushed the impulse to turn her around in his arms. Her tone hadn't implied she was toasty in the same way he was!

He stomped on the smoldering embers until every last libidinous thought was crushed to gray dust. After the near miss with the squid earlier, he'd ordered himself to behave the rest of the evening. His enticing neighbor was not as cool and collected as she'd like him to believe, but the next move was definitely hers.

His cell phone buzzed in his pants pocket. With a mental curse, he considered not answering. He was technically on vacation. Yet he could still get called in for a S.W.A.T. emergency.

Setting Carrie away from him, he took the cell from his pocket, glanced at the caller ID, and sighed. "I have to take this."

Carrie smiled and turned back to the panorama.

"What's wrong, Mama?" He kept his voice low, cognizant of all the people who stood within listening range.

"Who said anything was wrong? Can't I call my son for no good reason?"

Mama never did anything without a reason. He dug for patience. He loved his mother, but he wasn't in the mood to play *Twenty Questions* right now. "What's going on?"

"I need to know if you're coming to dinner tomorrow night."

He frowned. "My answer hasn't changed since this morning. I'm not sure if I'll make it down to Colorado Springs at all this weekend."

Watching Carrie's hair lift on a breeze, he could think of a hundred things he'd rather be doing than attending one of his mother's bi-monthly dinner parties with all of her friends from the old neighborhood. All of those things centered around the woman in front of him. He wanted to bury his nose in Carrie's scented hair. He longed to touch every inch of her satiny skin. He hungered to wrap himself in her heat over and over again.

Goosebumps rose on her neck above her jacket and, for a second, he thought she'd read his mind. Then a gust of wind dashed between them and flattened her silk pants against her legs. She shivered. Automatically reaching out to wrap an arm around her, he realigned their bodies to share his heat with her. A mistake, since he almost forgot he was talking to his mother.

"Giacobbe? Are you still there?"

"Yes," he said, distracted by the way Carrie's curved backside cradled him. "Look, Mama, I'm in the middle of something right now. You always make plenty of spaghetti so what's the problem if I show up or not?"

"I hoped...*non importa.*" When he didn't respond, she sighed dramatically in his ear. "That *brutto* wallpaper can wait until next week, Giacobbe."

It took him a few seconds to remember he'd told her his plan to strip the second spare bedroom this weekend. Then he registered his mother's descent into her native tongue revealing her frustration with his non-cooperation. An alarm went off in his head. Tomorrow night's dinner was a smoke screen. She hadn't gotten to the real reason for the phone call yet.

He lost interest in pursuing her intentions when a tendril of Carrie's soft hair lifted on another breeze and brushed across his lips. His lungs filled with the intoxicating scent of carnations and woman. A groan almost slipped from his mouth into his mother's ear. "I have to go," he said huskily. "I'll call you tomorrow."

"But—"

"Bye, Mama," he said, cutting her off.

He knew he'd pay for that later, but his mother was the least of his problems right now. If he didn't subdue his impulses, Carrie would soon feel how deeply she affected him. He didn't want to scare her off.

Turning off his phone so his mother couldn't interrupt again, he tucked it into his pants pocket. The move put an inch of the cool night air between his body and Carrie's, but he was unable to force himself to let go of her waist. "Sorry about that," he said over her head.

"Problem?"

Maybe below his belt, but he wasn't about to reveal that!

"No. That was my mother. I guess I didn't answer one of her questions sufficiently this morning."

"It's nice you talk to your mom."

"Not every woman would agree with you." He chuckled. "Dad's been gone a while, but I'm her only child and my move from Colorado Springs to Riverton was hard on her. I fell into the habit of talking to her on the phone every day. Sometimes, it's more than once a day. Guess that makes me a mama's boy."

Carrie laughed and snuggled into him, eliminating the space between them. "Not necessarily. I had an Italian friend in high school that was very close to his family, especially his mother. He was also captain of the football team and no one would have dared to call him a 'mama's boy'. I envied him his huge family. They were always there for each other.

"There's nothing wrong with caring about your mother. She must be lonely without you."

Jake didn't want to hear the longing in her voice because it made him wonder if her "friend" was actually more than that. "Mama still has most of her friends nearby, but she lost her driver's license last year thanks to failing eyesight. She can't come to Riverton now unless someone drives her."

"I gather it's been a while since you visited."

He shrugged. "I've been putting in a lot of hours at the station. Moving. It's been hard to get away." All valid excuses. However, the truth is he wasn't ready to deal with his mother's questions about his break up with Daniela so he'd been avoiding any conversation beyond their brief phone calls for almost four months. He had a feeling his time was running out.

Carrie stirred in his embrace. "Speaking of family, Jake, we'd better head back now. I have to pick up Eric first thing in the morning. He's got an entire day of baseball scheduled, and it's getting late."

Jake tensed. Eric wasn't coming home at all tonight? Great. Just great. There was nothing he'd like more than to rush Carrie home and follow up on his own inclinations. Whether she was ready or not. Whether he was. His repeated cautions to himself had done little to quench his potent physical response to her. Simply holding her was an exquisite torture that left him aching.

"I thought Eric wasn't allowed to sleep over at Davy's for a while," he said roughly."

Carrie moved away to take a last look at the city lights. Her voice wafted around him on a capricious breeze. "He is grounded, but I figured it would be too late to pick him up tonight so I let him stay."

Jake's eyes shut against the possibilities that immediately slammed into his brain. The remnants of Carrie's spiced floral fragrance clung to his jacket and dragged at his resistance like a pair of smoky hands that carried cartoon characters mindlessly into danger. How was he to take her home now—knowing the one serious barrier to his desire, Eric, was not in place—and still walk away?

Carrie turned from the panorama toward the parked car. "Jake? You ready?" she called over her shoulder as she started to walk away.

Watching the feminine sway of her petite body, satiny skin sliding beneath silk, Jake swallowed hard. He jammed his hands into his pants pockets and trailed behind her, his answer audible only to himself. "There's ready...and ready."

He was damned if they meant the same thing.

Chapter Five

It wasn't until Carrie began to recognize landmarks near home that she acknowledged the evening was ending too soon to suit her. It had been ages since she'd had so much fun, and Jake rested at the heart of that enjoyment. Somehow, he'd managed to push all the right buttons without setting off any of her hair-trigger alarms.

Okay. There were a couple of near misses.

She was grateful he hadn't noticed her unruly response to him when he picked her up at the house. It also wasn't his fault she got all hot and bothered watching him eat. That craziness could be chalked up to the power of her loneliness. Six years was a long time to remain celibate. She was bound to have the occasional twinge of sexual awareness. It was squelched quickly enough so it appeared the date wasn't such a bad idea after all.

At least she now knew she could live with Jake. As a neighbor, that is. The two of them did have more than a street address in common. They both enjoyed the classics, comedies, and old monster films. Adventure stories were their favorite read. Even their political beliefs were compatible, although they agreed to disagree on the way to solve some of society's more pressing problems. How Jake could remain in police work and still have so much faith in human nature was a mystery to her.

Carrie examined his profile in the dim light from the Mustang's dashboard. The uncompromising thrust of his chin. His slightly crooked nose. The reckless fall of dark hair on his forehead. Jake's profile, as well as his personality, was a study in contrasts. A fascinating combination of strength and tenderness, confidence and vulnerability.

"We're home," he said, pulling into his driveway.

Dragged from her reverie, she watched him walk around to assist her out of the car. With his large hand cupped around her elbow, he strode across the street. She had to take two steps to his one and, in no time, they came to a stop outside her front door.

Jeez. What was the rush? All of a sudden, Jake had become a stranger. Under the glowing porch light, his eyes looked calm enough—unreadable, in fact—but somehow, she sensed an edginess in his stiff stance.

"Do you have your keys?"

She handed them over and, within seconds, the front door was open and Jake was again standing two feet away.

His hasty retreat had the oddest effect on her. While she should be happy he didn't seem to expect the requisite goodnight kiss of a real date, she only felt rejected. It was unnerving to know the woman inside her was still willing to court emotional chances.

Remember what happened the last time you jumped off that particular cliff.

The mental reminder was unwelcome, but it moved her to action. "Good night, Jake." She leaned up to brush a kiss against his jaw.

It was a mistake, of course. The stream of electricity that arced from his skin to her lips caught her completely unprepared. It jolted sluggish nerve endings to life and randomly short-circuited what remained of her brain cells. Her legs unsteady, she searched his face.

It was surprisingly blank. Except for his eyes. They were no longer calm. Far from it. They were now dark and turbulent and fixed on her with hot intensity.

Only a fool played with fire, but she couldn't help but wonder what would happen if she walked into the flames. Would they warm her or burn her to a crisp? The only way to know was to kiss him again.

Did she dare? How could she not? This was their one and only date, wasn't it? She'd never get another chance.

"Good night, Carr—"

Her lips cut off Jake's words and, for an instant, the heavenly feel of his mouth melding with hers was enough to quench her curiosity. His heat thawed her insides, filled the cold, empty spaces in her heart. It raced to keep up with the electrical impulses zipping through her body.

When she realized their lips were their sole point of contact even though she stood on her tiptoes to reach his mouth, she swayed into his body. "Jake?"

Carrie's husky plea against his mouth, her taste, the feel of her yielding curves burrowing into his hard length...Jake couldn't hold out against the relentless assault on his fractured senses. He'd wanted her to take the next step. She had and, damn his clamoring libido, he craved more.

Lowering his head, he took what he needed. His arms surrounded her, lifting her into his body until they meshed from chest to thigh. Her lips parted on a gasp of surprise, of acceptance. She wriggled against him. He groaned his approval.

His tongue thrust past the edges of her teeth, probing deeply. Without preliminary, without hesitation. He plundered her sweetness as he blindly pushed into the house, carrying her with him. He didn't stop moving until they bumped into one of the entry walls.

Caught between two equally unyielding surfaces, Carrie moaned and dropped her purse to the floor. He kicked it aside and tossed the ring of keys that bit into his left hand after it. Reluctant to drag himself away from her drugging kisses, he sucked air into his starved lungs. "I didn't mean, we shouldn't, ah, hell."

Recapturing her lips, he eased back so she could slide down his body. His hands gentled, trailed caresses along her spine beneath her jacket until they came to rest on her backside. With a low, tortured sound, he ground his erection intimately into her softness to alert her to his tenuous hold. "Carrie, honey," he groaned at last, "tell me to stop."

"Mmm." Carrie responded to the rumble of his deep voice with an instinctive, feminine moan. Stop this? It had been too long since a man held her, made her feel so alive. So desirable and, oh, so desperately needy. Never had she encountered such a burning need to get near someone.

To alleviate the problem, she dragged her hands from his thick hair and worked her way down until she discovered a gap in his jacket. She dove inside where taut muscles rippled against her palms. The soft feel of only one thin layer of cotton between her fingertips and his naked skin set off tremors deep in her belly. Moving forward, she touched —

Something cold.

Something hard.

As if stung, she jerked both hands out of Jake's jacket away from the holster tucked high against his body. "You're wearing a gun?"

He trailed kisses along her jaw. "I always wear one," he said, the words distant, unfocused, against her ear.

She tilted her head to grant him better access to the tender skin beneath her earlobe. Then harsh memories reverberated through her head like a sledgehammer, knocking down the walls of desire she'd been building like an ingenuous child with a new set of blocks.

What are you doing? Jake's a cop. He wears a gun. Even on a date. The man's a walking, talking risk, and your risk-taking days are long gone. She gulped for air to smother the panic.

"Carrie?"

Her brain barely functioned, but she knew she had to escape the question forming in his too sexy, hot chocolate eyes. She pushed him back several steps so he once again stood on her doorstep. "Good-bye, Jake," she choked out before closing the door in his face.

Refusing to listen when he called her name, she locked the deadbolt with nerveless fingers and backed up until she knew she was far enough away to resist the temptation to reopen the door. To her house. Or to her heart.

~~~

Giving in to her feminine curiosity had to be one of those more reckless impulses she'd forsworn years ago, Carrie decided later Saturday. Sagging in her office chair, she massaged her temples. No. Agreeing to go out with Jake in the first place was the truly questionable move. Who knew the man would tap into a cavernous well of desire that even she hadn't known existed?

As much as she'd adored her husband, she'd never felt an all-consuming passion when he made love to her. Tomás was an innately gentle, considerate man, and it was reflected in the slow, tender way he touched her. Her youth and inexperience, not to mention her basic insecurities at the time, hadn't helped. The sad truth was she'd never reached for a man with pure, unadulterated lust on her mind.

Until last night. Until Jake.

How could one man reduce her to such a state so easily? Lost in a sensual mist, she'd forgotten everything. Her past. Her memories. Her solemn promise to protect the broken pieces of her heart. It had taken the cold, hard reality of Jake's gun to remind her of the danger he represented and that's what disturbed her the most. The *necessity* of that reminder.

She'd jeopardized her peace of mind, and for what? She hadn't even talked to Jake about Eric's brush with gangs, which was the reason she'd accepted the date in the first place.

Staring at her computer screen, Carrie deleted the last two lines of gibberish she'd added to the Forensen's lease document. If only it were possible to erase last night's fiasco with a push of a button. Steamy fantasies of what might have happened had she not come to her senses plagued her mind all day. She'd been running around the office in a perpetual state of arousal.

She squirmed in her chair. It didn't help to dwell on the fact long abstinence had clearly turned her into a sex-starved nymphomaniac. So, she'd embarrassed herself and dented the emotional wall she'd crawled behind after her husband died. She had to put the date, Jake, her longing for one more touch, one more kiss from her mind. Distractions, no matter how temporary, were the last thing she needed.

By year's end, sooner if the building was finished on time, Sam planned to open a new office north of Riverton in Brighton. It was imperative he chose her to manage it. All her thoughts must be centered on sales, sales, and more sales if she wanted to secure her future with O'Reilly Realty. With Eric growing so fast, she couldn't wait much longer to look seriously at a college fund.

There wasn't room in her life for any man, cop or not. If her hormones could wait twenty-nine years before suddenly going amok, they could just shut back down for another thirty. Another painful relationship wasn't on her agenda. Ever.

"Hey, Carrie, it's a clear day outside. When do you plan to come out of that fog of yours?"

Startled to see her boss standing in her office doorway, she summoned a smile. "Did you need something, Sam?"

"Do you have the file on the Morrison house?"

"The Morrison house?"

"You know, the second one we went through this morning. It has that hundred year old cottonwood tree in the front yard."

She didn't want to admit her frazzled brain had connected the giant tree to the Silverman's house. The Silvermans had the Victorian with the wraparound porch. Or did they?

Carrie gave up and riffled the folders in front of her, then handed one over the desk. "Here it is. Sorry I didn't get it back to you." She'd accomplished nothing today. Thankfully, Sam hadn't noticed her preoccupation.

"No problem." He took one of the visitor seats placed strategically in front of her desk and studied her until she began to fidget. "Want to talk?"

He'd noticed.

She picked up her pen to doodle on her desk blotter. "There's nothing to talk about."

"Joan warned me you'd be this way."

"What way?"

"Give me a break. Joan said you'd be a basket case today and she was right." Sam tapped the Morrison folder against his knee, frowned. "You can talk to me, Carrie. Maybe you think I don't understand, but Tomás was my best friend. I want to help. I know what you're feeling right now."

He didn't have a clue what she was feeling. She stared with dismay at the row of expanding red-ink hearts that had magically appeared on her blotter. She'd kissed a cop and liked it entirely too much. What was worse, she wanted to do it again.

Feeling desire rise like a tide that might never recede, she threw down the pen and rose from her chair. She turned away to stare aimlessly out the window at the traffic passing by the building.

Sam cleared his throat behind her. "Carrie, it's not disloyal to have feelings for someone else, to be attracted to another man. It's been six years. Tomás wouldn't want you to spend the rest of your life alone."

"Whoa, Sam, slow down," she said, facing him with a small laugh. "It was only a date. No big deal." Her fingers crossed behind her back.

"You also have prime beachfront property on the Alaska tundra I've just got to see to believe, huh?" He shook his head in defeat, stood, and glanced down at her blotter. "Carrie," he said, "please remember, if you need anything, you know, if you need to talk to a man about, um, just call, okay?"

Her agitation eased at his stumbling efforts to help. Although she wanted to strangle him sometimes for his chauvinistic tendencies, she knew he cared about her. "Sam, you're one of my best friends. I couldn't have survived the last six years without you. I do appreciate everything you've done for me and Eric. But—"

"I can keep my big nose out of it." Sam nodded, grinned. "Okay, okay. Some things I can't do as a friend." He grabbed her purse from the corner of the desk where she'd tossed it and thrust it into her hands. "As your boss, however, you have to listen to me. It's dinner time, for crying out loud. Go home and feed my godson."

~~~

"Eric!" Jake jogged the last few feet to meet up with Carrie's son walking home from the stop sign where he was dropped off by the silver SUV he remembered from the night before. "That Davy's mom who dropped you off?"

"Hi, Jake." He shifted a baseball glove from hand to hand. "Yeah, Mrs. O'Reilly had carpool this week."

Jake motioned toward the glove. "Practice?"

Eric scowled. "Nah. We had a game this afternoon."

"Not good, huh?"

"We won. Seven to two."

His mission momentarily sidetracked in the face of

Eric's dejection, Jake stared. "I'm confused. That sounds like a pretty good score to me."

One rather beat up tennis shoe scraped at the sidewalk. "Yeah, well, I didn't get any of the points."

"That's the way it goes sometimes."

"I never get any. It's a real bummer."

Jake gazed into eyes identical to Carrie's, in color and in vulnerability. "Why not?"

"I can't hit the ball."

He smiled sympathetically. "You just have to practice more."

"Do you know how to play baseball?"

"Sure."

"Could you teach me?"

Jake examined the kid's hopeful expression, less taken aback by the request than his serious consideration of it. Eric should take this sort of thing to his father. The problem was, he didn't have one and Jake couldn't forget that fact. The boy hadn't been far from his thoughts since he caught him in his backyard earlier in the week. Every time he laid eyes on him, he experienced a disquieting sense of déjà vu, even though he'd decided it was only Eric's build and hair color that reminded him of Mateo.

That hadn't prevented his protective instincts from kicking in with a vengeance with Eric. He'd gone to the kid's school yesterday to talk to the officer, Bernie Bates, assigned there and was relieved to discover the group Eric and Davy wanted to join wasn't actually a gang. They were simply six graders trying to get rid of second graders who were pestering them. Jake and Bates talked with the older kids about finding other ways to deal with youngsters who looked up to them. He'd walked out of the school knowing he'd done what he could for Eric, as the kid's father would have done if he were alive.

"Eric, I haven't picked up a bat in a long time, but let me think about it. Okay? You might be better off working with your coach."

Besides, your mother probably won't let me near you after what I did last night.

Although he didn't look convinced, Eric nodded.

Reminded of why he stood on the street in front of his neighbor's house, his figurative hat in his hands, Jake straightened. "Is your mom home?"

"She should be home from work." The boy walked across the lawn. "Come on. I'll find her."

Determined to assess the damage his uncivilized behavior had caused to his relationship with Carrie, Jake entered the house behind Eric. They spotted her in the backyard. Jake lingered within the protection of the kitchen while his companion ran through the open double-glass doors to the patio.

Eric joined his mother next to the barbecue grill. "Hey, Mom."

She grinned. "Hey, kiddo. How'd you do?"

"Lousy. Maybe I shoulda gone for soccer instead."

"Aw, honey, that's too bad." She dropped the barbecue grate over aluminum-wrapped shapes that looked like ears of corn and raised one eyebrow. "Think a cheeseburger will help?"

"Yeah, but what I really need is more practice. Jake says so."

"Jake?"

Carrie's gaze locked on him as he stepped into view. "I ran into Eric out front."

"Jake. Hello." She straightened. "What can we—"

Her gaze followed Eric's progression back into the house. "Um, I. What can I do for you?"

He drew nearer, lowered his voice. "First, you can stop looking at me like I'm a cat burglar after your good silver."

"Oh, but I don't—"

Jake almost smiled at the startled look on her face. She was so damned enticing when she got flustered. "I'm here to apologize for something I did last night."

She flushed. "That's not necessary."

He shook his head. "I'm afraid it is. My gun has been such an integral part of me for so long, it never occurred to me it might freak you out. For that, I apologize."

The shadows in her eyes lightened. "Oh, I thought you were sorry for..."

Her lashes dropped to hide her feelings, but Jake saw excitement flare for one, too-brief instant. Her mouth softened as if beneath his again, as if they could pick up where they left off the previous night. It was what drew him over here this evening. The contradictions. Puzzles intrigued him. The one Carrie presented promised to drive him crazy.

He'd screwed up when he kissed her last night. She'd started it. She'd demanded his response. Not that he'd needed much coaxing. Not that he was complaining either. What had sparked between them was unexpected, unbelievable, and gone too soon. He wanted it back. He wanted to know why she ran hot one minute, cold the next. He *wanted*. That's all there was to it. "Do you accept my apology?"

She nodded.

"Good." He grinned. "I can ask my favor then."

"Favor?" Carrie coughed when the smoke from the

grill enveloped her head, but she couldn't move without bumping into him. She waved her hand in the air and nearly swiped him in the nose. "Sure, if I can help."

Jake moved away to lean negligently against one of the wooden posts holding up the patio cover. He watched with interest as she calculated how far he'd retreated before she stepped out of her smoky circle. Then, he pressed on. "It's occurred to me I've been in my new house almost three weeks now and I haven't met any of my neighbors. Besides you and Eric." He flashed another smile. "I'm hoping you'll help me out. You know, introduce me around."

"Well—"

"It's short notice, but I thought I'd have a barbecue at my place tomorrow. Do you think you could scrounge up a few people?"

Jake saw the struggle on her face. Surely she won't feel threatened with her friends around her? Besides, he'd accomplish several goals with his hastily formed plans. He'd meet his neighbors and assess the gang influence in his new neighborhood, get back in Carrie's good graces, and surround himself with so many people he wouldn't dream of pushing her any faster than she wanted to go. Why was she balking?

"How many did you have in mind?"

Probably not enough, he speculated, eyeing her hip hugging, black stretch pants and oversized scarlet T-shirt. She barely looked old enough to vote, yet this outfit did as much damage to his over-stimulated libido as what she wore last night. "Five or six couples? I want to get to know people, not just learn a bunch of names I can't remember."

Carrie set the grill cover in place. "I guess I could

ask Joan and Sam, although they're not technically neighbors since they live on the river two streets over. Then, there are the Pattersons. They live to the right of you."

"Just don't ask the Lawrences, Mom," Eric cut in from his position on top of the picnic table. He took a swig from a sweat-beaded can of soda.

Jake was disconcerted to have missed the boy's return. "Why not?"

He shot a look at his mother. "They're okay, I guess, but Mrs. Lawrence makes the grossest stuff. You'd know who she was real fast 'cause you'd be throwing up all over the place."

"Eric!" Carrie exclaimed.

"That bad, huh?"

"The worst."

"Eric Tomás Padilla!" The motherly warning was stronger this time.

The boy stared at his hands, his head bowed. "Well, it's true," he muttered under his breath.

"That's all right, kid." Jake laughed. "Your mom can invite the Lawrences. This lady I have to meet." He eased away from the post. "Besides, I'm cooking so you don't have to fear for your life. Okay?"

When he nodded, Carrie laughed. "Honey, I don't suppose it's occurred to you Jake might not be able to cook either."

His stricken look was answer enough. Jake grinned, Carrie's lighthearted laughter tugging delicately at his heightened senses. "I can cook, Eric," he said, not looking at the boy.

She stared back. "What time should I tell everyone? Oh, and we are talking children too, right? Families?"

As long as she and Eric came, Jake didn't care if everyone brought their pets along. "Three o'clock and kids, too. I just need a total in the morning so I can plan."

"That's a lot of mouths to feed. Do you need any help?"

He didn't plan to be in the same kitchen alone with Carrie for any length of time without another taste of her lips, so that nixed that. "No, I'll make it simple. If I need help when everyone arrives, I'll yell."

Chapter Six

"Why do I keep doing these stupid things?" Carrie paced the living room in front of her best friend several hours later. Night had fallen. Her son had gone to bed. The end of her world loomed ahead and she could do nothing to stop it.

"You want my opinion?" Joan sat cross-legged on the couch like a swami about to impart her great wisdom on the clueless masses. "I think you've gone off the deep end. It's great."

Carrie paced faster. "That's the best you can do? I know I'm certifiable. I could have told you that the instant I kissed the man."

Joan studied the bright coral enamel on her fingernails. "Since you said Jake wasn't in that group named in the police report and you can't remember ever seeing him before, I don't see your problem."

"You don't see my problem?" Carrie stopped dead in her tracks, unable to move as she looked down at her friend. "You're crazier than I am. Jake's still a—"

"Man!" Joan interrupted forcefully. "He's only a man, Carrie. One of the things you've never come to grips with is that even policemen put their pants on one leg at a time. Just like every other male you know. The bonus is this one flips your switch and lights your fuse."

Wrapping her arms around her body, Carrie tried not to think about the way Jake put his pants on. That led to picturing him taking them off and —

"Wait a minute. Weren't you the one who questioned my dating Jake in the first place?"

"Someone had to play Devil's Advocate so you'd analyze what you were doing." Her friend shrugged. "You've been hiding behind your excuses too long, in any case. The only way you'll get on with your life is if you give up this idea you're better than the rest of us because you don't need anyone else."

Stunned by the harsh assessment, her arms dropped to her sides. "What an awful thing to say."

Joan winced. "I'm sorry, sweetie. I know that hurts, but it's time you face facts. This has little to do with what Jake does for a living. You just won't admit you might need someone besides yourself to be happy."

Carrie opened her mouth, but Joan wouldn't let her interrupt. She waved her hand. "No, let me say this. For years, I've hoped you'd wake up and see the flaw in your attitudes. I'm not waiting any longer." She tugged on Carrie's arm, forcing her to sit beside her. "Carrie, we've known each other, what, nineteen years?"

"Since second grade."

"I've watched you push people away all these years," she said with a nod. "You've lived in a vacuum every day I've known you. Until you met Tomás, I thought you'd always be that way."

The aching sense of loss that automatically surfaced when she thought of her husband raced through her. Sweet, caring Tomás. He'd been the calm in the center of the storm that was her life as a senior in high school. When her mother gave up her fight against cancer three days after Carrie graduated, he'd been the one to quietly pick up the pieces. That was the day she'd foolishly fallen in love.

"Oh, sure. Loving Tomás didn't get me very far. He left me, just like everyone else I've ever cared for."

Joan sat back, a satisfied expression on her face. "Do you hear what you're saying? He didn't die on purpose. It was an accident. You know it was. He was in the wrong place, at the wrong time."

She placed a restraining hand on Carrie's instant retreat. "He didn't leave you voluntarily, honey. You've admitted as much in your more analytical moments. You know, those times when you actually allow yourself to think about the things that distress you.

"As for the rest, forget it. I know how lonely it is to be shuffled from one relative to the next when you're a child who can't understand divorce and necessity. Be grateful you weren't in foster care. Anyway, I thought you settled all this with your mother before she died."

Carrie rose from the sofa, her arms hugged tight around her waist. Joan *would* drag out her psychology degree now. "I did," she admitted. "That last few months with Mom was healing. For both of us, I think. But, a lifetime of abandonment isn't that easy to forget."

"I know," Joan replied as she, too, rose to her feet. "If you're not careful, though, you're going to make your son as paranoid of developing friendships as you are. Watching you, he'll learn to not let anyone in. You've worked too hard to avoid that. Don't blow it now."

"I've got friends," she said in her defense. "I have Eric."

Joan rose and walked across the living room to hug

her. "Yeah, you've got friends. Good ones, if I do say so myself." She smiled crookedly. "But that's not what I'm talking about, and you know it. Don't forget you owe something to yourself, too. You can't look to Eric forever for companionship. Someday, you're going to have to let him go and find your own life. Otherwise, you'll shrivel up and die of loneliness."

She couldn't deal with the same old argument they'd had for years. "Joan, please."

"Oh, please yourself. You think I haven't been listening? I've heard enough to know this cop of yours has sparked something powerful and passionate inside you. You're out of your mind if you think you can simply ignore it." She smiled briefly, patted her cheek, and walked to the front door to open it.

"Wait!" Carrie ran after her. "I'm sorry. I don't want to argue." She shrugged helplessly. "I promise to think about what you said. Okay? Please say you'll come to the barbecue."

You don't need to ask, sweetie." She smiled. "Despite what you think right now, I am your friend. You can always count on me for support. Sam and I'll go to Jake's barbecue. We wouldn't miss this one for the world."

Her friend's observations haunted Carrie long after Joan left. Deep down, Carrie knew she was right. She hadn't been able to ignore anything about her all-too-masculine neighbor since she'd laid eyes on the man. No matter how many times she reminded herself that he was a cop, the last kind of man she should want in her life after what happened to Tomás, she couldn't seem to resist the dangerous allure that surrounded Jake either. Her blood raced, hot and heavy, at the thought of the fire in his eyes, the zing of his kiss. Even the rumble of his deep voice as he spoke about inconsequential things last night sent her senses reeling. Yet every time he touched her, he also made her feel safe and protected.

"That doesn't mean you should give in to your impulses," she whispered. That direction led to certain heartache. The only reason she was maintaining contact with Jake was because of Eric, and she'd be a fool to forget that fact. Somehow, she had to chase her rebellious needs back into hibernation so Jake Stefani didn't take the last small pieces of her shattered heart with him when they inevitably went their separate ways.

Because God knows, with her track record, there was no doubt they'd go their separate ways.

~~~

Sunday morning was a murky gray destined to deepen any anxieties Carrie awakened with, but she pushed her worries aside and jumped out of bed. She had something to prove to Joan, to herself and one way or another today was the day to prove it.

Dissecting her uninhibited response to Jake's kiss Friday night was a waste of time. It was a fluke of nature, complicated by a lack of male companionship and too much night air and wine. Her instantaneous, insane desire to rip the man's clothes off when she saw him step into her backyard last night didn't mean anything either.

Desire tended to lose its punch when ignored long enough and, if Joan were to be believed, Carrie was the queen of restraint. She could handle an acquaintance, her new watchword, with the man. She was self-sufficient and liked it that way. Everyone's clothing could just stay put.

Eric's needs were different though. Carrie might not be able to replace his father, but she could give him every scrap of her love and make sure there were good men to influence his life. She'd develop friendships all day long if it meant giving Eric everything he deserved.

Despite her mental pep talk, it took her until nine o'clock to cross the street to Jake's house. Wiping damp palms on her turquoise jeans, she knocked. "Hi, Jake," she began when the door opened.

Her mouth snapped shut when she saw his scowl. Uh-oh. Maybe a phone call was a better idea. Jake looked rumpled, like he'd slept in his clothes and wasn't particularly happy about it.

His whole manner changed in the next instant. "Carrie." His smile flowed over her like thick honey. "Good morning."

"I'm sorry if I'm too early," she said, "but you wanted a list of your guests. I hope I didn't drag you out of bed." She found herself gauging how difficult it might be to drag him back there.

"You didn't. I've been waiting for you."

Carrie got lost somewhere between the intimacy of his smile and the confidence in his chocolate brown eyes. Then, aware her behavior was just short of adolescent, she prompted, "You do still want to have a barbecue, don't you?"

Glancing over his shoulder, Jake hesitated, then shrugged. "Come on in."

With that gracious invitation, Carrie considered going home and calling later. She wished she had when she stepped into the house and was immediately pinned down under the penetrating gaze of the Italian woman who stood in the center of the entry, her fists on her ample waist.

Painfully aware she'd apparently stepped into the middle of an argument, Carrie apologized again. "I'm sorry. I'm intruding. This is obviously not a good time."

Before she could retreat, Jake cupped his hand around her elbow to stop her. "You're not intruding," he assured her. His gaze locked on the older woman. "Mama and I will finish our talk later. Won't we?"

It didn't sound as if he'd take no for an answer and, oddly enough, both his words and his presence at her side made Carrie believe he'd placed himself between the two of them on purpose. Who was he protecting? And why?

Throwing up her hands in a classic gesture, the other woman spouted a short barrage of Italian at the ceiling. When she ran down, her gaze fixed on Carrie. "So, Giacobbe, you wish to introduce me to your friend?"

He was frowning at his mother so Carrie wondered what the woman had said, but he performed the introductions like nothing had happened. "Mama," he said. "This is my neighbor, Carrie Padilla. Carrie, this is Fiona Stefani, my mother."

The older woman crossed the hardwood floor to shake Carrie's hand. "Pleased to meet you."

Carrie had a feeling the vote was still out on that one. Her anxiety level rose another notch, a perfectly ridiculous reaction since it mattered not one whit if Jake's mother liked her. "About the barbecue," Carrie said, focusing on her purpose for standing in Jake's foyer. "How's seventeen?"

"Seventeen."

Watching carefully, she decided he wouldn't really turn tail and run. It wasn't as if she'd told him to jump off a cliff in a straitjacket or anything equally questionable. "You said to invite five or six couples. It was kind of late notice so I only found four available, the Pattersons, Lawrences, O'Reillys, and the Smiths. But with myself, Eric, and the rest of the children, it still comes to seventeen."

She smiled at the wary look in his eyes. Now, she was the one to feel protective. "Don't worry about feeding all of us. I've already arranged with everyone to bring something." She paused. "What were you planning?"

"I have several cut-up chickens to barbecue, but I was waiting to talk to you about numbers before I went to the store for anything else."

"Just plan on the chicken you already have. We've got everything else covered."

"What exactly does that mean?"

"You provide the chicken. Between the rest of us there are hamburgers, baked beans, chips and dip, potato salad, cake and drinks." She waited, then provided with a straight face, "The Lawrences are bringing soft drinks."

He chuckled, sharing the inside joke. "Good. I'd hate to arrest Mrs. Lawrence for murder when we've barely met. If Eric hasn't exaggerated, her cooking ability is nothing short of criminal. As a police officer, it's my duty to protect all of my neighbors from danger."

Who would save her from that dangerously infectious smile of his? "You're all set, then," she said. "Do you need any help before three o'clock?"

Jake shook his head.

She addressed his mother, standing silently to one side, watching them. "I hope to see you at the barbecue, Mrs. Stefani."

"Mama, please. I'm Mama to everyone who knows me." Her dark eyes glittered as she raised an eyebrow at her son. "I'm not going anywhere for a few days, so I'll be delighted to join you." She escorted Carrie to the door, her arm draped around her back. "I'll even whip up a batch of my famous linguini for the occasion."

Thoroughly blindsided by Mama's beatific expression, Carrie allowed herself to be swept out of the house.

~~~

Jake confronted his mother the instant she turned away from the door, his arms crossed belligerently over his chest. He didn't like the familiar bulldog-with-a-bone look she'd adopted, any more than he'd liked finding her unannounced on his doorstep last night. But it was the way she'd just pushed Carrie out of his house that sharpened his tongue. "Okay, Mama, give it straight. What are you up to?"

She sailed past, patting his arm as she aimed for the kitchen. "Who says I'm up to anything?"

That innocent air didn't fool him. If he hadn't known she had something up her sleeve when she showed up last night towing Daniela behind her, her Italian rant about uncooperative sons to his dead father a few minutes ago would have given her away. The whole setup stank of Mama's matchmaking—or reconciliation scheme, in this case—and the smell would only get worse if he didn't do something about it. Fast.

He had no clue why Daniela would go along with whatever Mama had in mind, but there was no way his ex-girlfriend was there to reconcile with him. She wanted something. He'd be damned if he knew what it was since she'd taken everything, including his dog and self-respect, to Kansas City months ago.

He strode after his mother. "You said you and Daniela were only staying over so you can go shopping with Miss Eula and Miss Alba today."

The Cabrini twins were his dad's classmates and the first to welcome his new bride, Jake's mother, to Colorado Springs thirty-five years earlier. Ten years ago, they'd moved to their great-aunt's ancestral Riverton home to care for her until she died. They'd opened their home to Jake when he'd joined the Riverton Police. He'd only lived with them a few weeks, just long enough to find his own place to escape their matchmaking efforts managed he was sure by his mother seventy miles away.

"You are going shopping, right?"

She bent over to search through his half-empty cupboards. "That was the plan," she said, not looking at him.

That didn't sound good. "Was?"

She didn't respond, digging through his pots and pans with enough noise to wake the dead.

He had better luck interrogating bad guys! "It's not that you're not welcome, Mama, but you hate barbecues."

Unlike Jake's father, Mama had been raised in Italy before Lorenzo Stefani met her and moved her to America. As far as she was concerned, barbecues were an overrated American experience she could live without. The grill Lorenzo bought was used once by a neighbor, who'd kept it by default. Mama hadn't encouraged its return. Jake had to go to friends' homes to discover that he loved barbecue.

Mama glanced at the ceiling, removed a large soup pot from the cupboard, and slapped it down on the butcher block inset into the Spanish tile counter. "Don't raise your voice," she admonished. "You'll wake Daniela."

His irritation grew. As much as he loved his mother, there were times he'd rather wring her neck. He had a kink in his neck from camping on the living room floor after giving up his bed to his mother and Daniela, the loveseat Mama had insisted on giving him far too short for comfort. The thought of his ex-girlfriend lying where he'd pictured Carrie sharpened his resolve. "Tell me the real reason you're here."

His mother sighed. "You were supposed to come to dinner last night, and you canceled. Daniela was back from Kansas City, so I asked her to bring me here. I knew if I talked to you on the phone, I wouldn't get answers." She shrugged, hurt in her eyes. "It was too late for Daniela to drive us on to Eula and Alba's house, you know. They're in bed by nine o'clock every night."

Since they'd arrived on his doorstep after eleven o'clock, Jake knew they had no intention of going any further than his front door when they'd left Colorado Springs. But he didn't call her on it because he also knew it was his fault she'd felt compelled to take drastic action.

He lowered himself into a kitchen chair, remorse pricking his conscience. He'd been unwilling to face her inevitable questions about his breakup with Daniela, so he'd spent the past four months making excuses for not visiting. Their daily phone calls didn't give her enough time to probe. With an empty month to fill and a need to smooth her ruffled feathers, he'd decided he'd put it off long enough. But then, he'd met Carrie and the furthest he wanted to travel was across the street.

Catching his mother watching him, he frowned. "You couldn't have missed me, Mama. How many sat down to dinner last night? Twenty?" The number had grown since his mother lost her driver's license last year thanks to degenerating eyesight. Now, most of her friends came to her.

She mumbled something indistinct under her breath.

He stiffened in his seat. "Say that again."

"It was only Daniela, okay? She came to me in the hope of seeing you. I knew you'd be upset if I gave her your address over the phone."

"But it's okay to sideswipe me with her at dinner." The last of Jake's guilt evaporated as he sat back and glared at her. "Then, when that didn't work you dragged her to my front door in the middle of the night."

"I don't know what happened between you two," Mama said, "but I'm sure if you talk to each other, you can fix whatever is wrong. You don't want to throw your marriage away over a misunderstanding."

"We never discussed marriage."

Mama sniffed indelicately. "You would have made an honest woman of her eventually. That can still happen now that she wants to talk to you."

Marry Daniela? Not a chance in hell. She'd been quite clear about what she didn't want when she ran off to Kansas City. Jake topped the list. He was grateful to her now for releasing him from his mistake so he could move on, literally and figuratively.

He couldn't say that to his mother, though, without setting her off again. She'd set her heart on Daniela as the mother of his children, apparently not a dream she was prepared to give up without a fight. "I'll have to throw her in jail for harassment," he muttered, his head lowered. "It's the only way. No one will blame me once I explain the circumstances."

"Stop mumbling, Giacobbe. I can't hear you."

He laughed, his temper cooling as quickly as it flared. Mama was impossible and priceless. "You heard me just fine, and stop using my given name to intimidate me. It doesn't work anymore. I quit shaking in my boots when I was ten."

"Don't blame a mother for trying. We look after our sons the best we can."

"Which brings us back to why you dragged Daniela here. We're done. *I'm* done," he said pointedly.

"I thought, well, forget what I thought." Her head tilted, she studied him long enough to make him nervous. Then, she frowned. "Would it make a difference if I tell you she's moving back to Colorado Springs? Alone?"

He wasn't surprised to hear she'd left Colin. He'd given it less than a year before her dissatisfaction kicked in, but to voluntarily move back to her roots? Ever since she'd graduated high school and went to law school on a scholarship, she'd been running away from the trailer park where she'd grown up. Jake understood why she was never satisfied. That didn't mean he was the man to give her the happiness she sought. "She told you she wants to get back together?"

"Well, no. Not exactly." Mama waved a negligent hand. "She wants to talk though. What else could it be unless she realized her mistake? Maybe—"

He shook his head in warning before she could finish the thought. "I'm sorry things didn't work out for her in Kansas City, but that doesn't mean I'll take her back. I won't do that even for you."

"This neighbor of yours. She is married?"

The unexpected change of subject snapped his guard into place. "Carrie's a widow. But I am not, let me repeat this, *not* going to discuss her with you. How I pursue my woman is no concern of yours."

"Aha! I knew it!" Mama plopped down in the chair across from him, her gaze searching. "Is she your woman?"

Jake rose and stalked to the counter to pour himself a cup of coffee. He was a mature, thirty-year-old man who dealt with misguided souls every day. He was a fully trained member of a S.W.A.T. team designed to take down the most desperate criminals in the metro-Denver area. Handling one overly inquisitive Italian woman should be a piece of cake.

Shoulders hunched, he rubbed at an ache in his neck and remembered which Italian woman he was trying to manage. "We are not discussing this, Mama," he said, turning around to pin her under one of his stern policeman stares. "But, before we drop this subject, you have to understand something. You may come to this barbecue only if you swear to behave yourself and not interfere."

"Interfere? Me?" She looked at him with snapping, dark eyes, the perfect picture of affront. "I never interfere."

She rose and went back to the stove, muttering to herself. "But a little help never goes amiss, Giacobbe

Marcos Stefani."

Jake stared at his mother's squared backside and shuddered in his sneakers.

Chapter Seven

The barbecue was in full swing when Joan sidled up to Carrie, a devilish light in her green eyes. "Did you know there are books stacked four feet deep behind the shower curtain in the downstairs bathtub?"

Carrie laughed. "Joan, I can't take you anywhere. Hasn't anyone told you, it's bad manners to snoop?" Scanning the activity in Jake's back yard, she acknowledged Sam's erratic wave of a spatula. "Besides, I already knew."

"There's got to be a story there. Give."

Joan's persistence made her cringe. "According to Mama, Jake was up all night trying to unpack three weeks' worth of boxes. He hasn't had a chance to fully move in. With company running in and out of his house, he had to tuck away some things."

"Mama told you all that?"

Holding up her fingers, she counted them off. "She also told me he can build anything, fix the plumbing, and cook Italian food to die for. He's a good provider and he'll make lots of beautiful bambinos with the right woman." Seeing the fist she'd made, she unwound her cramped fingers, one by one.

Joan bent over to pluck an iced soda from the round metal tub at their feet. "You sound remarkably calm for a woman who's been proposed to by a man's mother."

"Oh, no! It wasn't directed at me. Daniela Bertoni is the target." She nodded in the sultry woman's direction, right where she'd been all afternoon, wrapped around Jake like gauze. "Daniela was nearby when Mama was spouting off Jake's good points."

She told herself she was relieved by her interpretation of recent events. Yes. It had been disconcerting when Jake's ex-girlfriend greeted her at the door as his hostess. It wasn't like Carrie wanted to fill that role, despite the fact she'd organized everything for him. What did she care if Mama was encouraging their reunion? The woman was tall, voluptuous, and intelligent. With her career in criminal law, she'd make an excellent mate for Jake. She was also so friendly and likeable it was irritating.

Joan slurped her drink. "If you ask me, I think you should give the Italian Slinky a run for her money."

Carrie turned to shush her departing friend and caught a movement out of the corner of her eye. Jake had peeled away from his companion and headed in her direction, a solid set to his jaw. Butterflies took wing in Carrie's stomach. Deciding they had the right idea — flight, in any direction — she decided to do the same.

Glancing around, she looked for refuge. Joan joined Kitty Lawrence and Shirlee Patterson at the picnic table. All the kids not already eating were huddled around a big dirt pile Jake had in one corner, making an elaborate highway system for their cars and trucks. Sam O'Reilly and Harry Patterson flipped an ever-renewing batch of chicken and hamburgers on two separate grills under Mama's eagle eye. Roger Lawrence and Danny Smith had departed for the store to get more soft drinks.

Surrounded by people, there was nowhere to hide. Her options limited, she fled to the picnic table.

"Where's the fire?" Jake said into her ear a moment later. "I've been trying to catch you for an hour."

Braced against the blast of excitement racing through her bloodstream, she faced Jake and found him within easy kissing distance. She licked her dry lips. Darn it. How long would it take to forget how the man tasted?

Alarmed, she stared down at the heavy-duty paper plate that had somehow become folded between her fingers. "Pickles! We need pickles." She needed to pull herself together.

The order got louder as she looked up into simmering chocolate eyes. She tore her gaze away and rearranged the five pickle chips that remained on the plate. Then, she did it again. "Um. Why did you want me?" Why didn't the earth below her feet crack open, swallow her up, and crush her rebellious hormones to dust?

Jake didn't get a chance to respond.

"Hey, Carrie," Harry yelled from the grill area. "Where's that other bottle of barbecue sauce we brought over?"

Bless Harry!

Carrie smiled at her friend. "It's in the kitchen. I'll get it," she called out. Dashing away, she entered the house and spotted the bottle on the kitchen counter where she'd seen it earlier.

"Let me." Jake's hand brushed over her fingers. The bottle disappeared from sight. The kitchen door opened behind her. "Joan, would you take this to Harry? Joan?" There were heavy footsteps on the porch, then the door shut.

Carrie listened, but didn't hear anything beyond the click of the door latch. She slowly expelled the breath of air that she'd been holding. Jake had gone out. She was alone. Relaxing, she pushed her thumping heart back where it belonged then remembered she was supposed to replenish the pickles. She walked to the refrigerator.

"Where were we?" The voice was soft, achingly familiar.

"Jake!" The refrigerator door escaped her grip, slamming against the counter as she whirled around. Her hand trembled at her throat. "You scared the daylights out of me."

She avoided his eyes, but it didn't help her to think more clearly. All she could see were sleek muscles outlined in dark khaki slacks, a creamy white cotton shirt with the same problem. All that leashed masculine power called to her, despite her resolve to ignore it. She knew what Jake's hard body felt like pressed against hers. The memory was vivid enough to make her toes curl in her sandals.

He stepped closer. Too close. Before she could do anything constructive, she was cornered against the open refrigerator. "I didn't mean to frighten you, Carrie. I just haven't had a chance to talk with you since you arrived. I wanted to thank you."

"For what?"

One blunt finger stroked down her cheek. "You did a great job organizing my barbecue." He smiled. "I like your friends."

She worked to dampen the fire his brief touch had kindled. "They're your friends now, too." It wasn't surprising he fit in so well with the neighbors. He

99

seemed to know just the right thing to say to each of them. "Kitty Lawrence thinks you're the best thing to come along since sliced bread."

"That woman's a menace to society." He grimaced. "Does she even know what normal food is? Eric's been avoiding me since she had him lug in that casserole dish for her. The poor kid won't ever trust me again."

"Don't worry. Eric will forgive you anything since you promised to help him with his batting." A promise of tremendous concern. It was what she wanted, of course. For Eric. She, however, didn't trust herself enough to have more contact with Jake. "Anyway, you can tell him it's my fault. I forgot how much she likes to spring her creations on friends at parties."

"You aren't taking the rap," he said, resting a hand on top of the refrigerator door. "I'm no coward."

It was a good thing one of them wasn't cowardly. The instant she realized the last movement had brought him within inches of her, she shifted to one side to look over his shoulder. *Help!* "Where's Daniela?"

Jake frowned. "She'd better be outside, keeping Mama occupied. If she's not, all bets are off."

"Excuse me?"

His expression was grim. "My dear mother sicced Daniela on me, a presumption I can't take lightly. She just won't accept I'm not interested in being seduced."

"You're not?" Carrie was afraid her eyes were as big as the hole in her stomach. She must eat something. It was hunger she felt, not disappointment.

"I choose my own woman," he declared. He brushed a tendril of hair off her cheek and tucked it behind her ear, the light touch making her forget all about food. It was too hot to eat.

100

"Oh." Where did her wits go when this man was near? Shifting in place, she tried to expand on the space that had shrunk around her. "You made a bet with your girlfriend?"

"*Ex*-girlfriend," he clarified. "I'm afraid I used the wrong expression. What I meant was that Daniela and I made a deal. I forget today ever happened, and we can remain friends. She's being a friend right now and keeping Mama busy for me."

His gaze brushed here, lingered there, all over her face and neck until he settled on her eyes. "Mama will be dying to know what's going on in here. Not being able to find out will drive her up a wall." His voice was low, seductive, a mere wisp of sound.

Carrie swallowed convulsively, his clean male scent invading her lungs, robbing her of air. She barely noticed the refrigerator shelves digging into her backbone. What was the matter with her knees? Mama's famous linguini had more starch! "What is going on here?"

A light flickered in the depths of Jake's eyes. He leaned over and threw an arm around her. When his hand came back into view, he waved a jar between them. "I'm getting olives," he said. Humming to himself, he turned on his heel, walked to the door, unlocked it, and went outside.

Carrie was left with her mouth hanging open and a chill seeping through her skirt from the refrigerator behind her.

~~~

Jake walked the perimeter of his back yard until he spotted Sam's missing soft drink tub, tucked behind the dirt pile the kids had played in earlier. He grinned when

101

he saw the mixture of melted ice and dirt in the bottom. One submarine, half submerged, was all that remained of the muddy sea battle that had obviously taken place. Salvaging the derelict, he dumped the mud and stored the tub and toy under the porch for the night.

Scanning the yard, he policed the area again. The only remaining evidence that a barbecue had taken place was crushed grass, an empty picnic table, and Carrie's checked tablecloth. Jake stopped in his tracks and took the time to enjoy the sight of Carrie folding the red-and-white material into a tidy rectangle. His pleasure dimmed when she glanced up and he saw the wary look in her eyes.

What happened to the sweet gypsy who'd danced her way through his back yard all evening, tempting him abominably? Where was the delightful, outgoing woman who'd shared her friends? Carrie had locked that woman up, nice and tight. The ease with which she did that frustrated the hell out of him.

He hadn't waited patiently all day to get her to himself, only to have her snatch his opportunity away now. "Is that the last of it?" He indicated the tablecloth clutched in her arms.

"I think so."

He moved toward her. "Thanks for staying to help me clean up. I appreciate it."

"No problem." She stepped around the table in the direction of the porch and continued speaking without actually looking at him. "It's too bad your mother and Daniela had to leave. Weren't they supposed to stay a couple of days?"

Jake frowned. He recognized a diversionary tactic when he saw one. He just didn't understand it. No one had forced Carrie to stick around after the barbecue. Remaining behind had been her idea. "That was the plan. But Mama remembered something she had to do tomorrow, so Daniela took her home."

His ex-girlfriend would return in the next couple of days to drop off his German Shepherd, Riker, the real reason she'd wanted to talk to him. The dog had not taken his separation from Jake well and become more than she could handle. When she broke it off with Colin, her therapist had encouraged her to move back to Colorado Springs to deal with her family issues and she didn't have room for the dog in her apartment.

Not that she hadn't also tested the waters for a reconciliation. When he only took the dog back, she'd admitted sheepishly she'd known he wasn't the man for her almost from the start of their relationship but she'd been too scared of moving on. She'd then commented on his obvious attraction to Carrie and wished him the best. He'd hugged her and told her he hoped she'd find the happiness she was looking for, too. They'd parted on better terms this time around.

He touched Carrie's arm, slowing her progress to the back door. "Have a cup of coffee with me before you go," he suggested. "I'll make decaf."

"No, thanks," she said with a shake of her head. "It's after ten. I need to get Eric to bed. He has school in the morning."

"He's out cold on the loveseat in the living room. A few more minutes sleep won't hurt him."

Her feet settled on the first step. "I know, but—"

A sense of urgency prompted Jake into action. He clasped her around the waist, lifted her off the porch and into his arms. Where he wanted her to be. Where she belonged. "Stop running, Carrie."

Her spine stiffened against his palm. "I'm not running," she said. Her teeth caught on her lower lip.

His index finger traced her mouth until it trembled beneath his touch, then parted. "Yes, you are," he said. "You have been ever since we met."

The spicy scent of her floral perfume made him dizzy with longing. The heat radiating from her creamy skin set off a raging fire in his belly. The reckless power of her effect on him was disturbing. "Come on," he said. "Admit I'm right."

"No."

"Why not?"

"You're wrong," she said. "I don't have to run."

He tucked her tighter against him. "Then, you are as attracted as I am."

"No, I'm not."

His eyes narrowed at the challenge. "Your response is in your eyes when you look at me. It's in your body when I hold you." His head lowered until her mouth was a heartbeat away. "I taste it when I kiss you."

His lips brushed hers. Once. Twice. The third time, he deepened the caress drawing strength on the attraction she denied. It was there. She only had to acknowledge it.

With a long, low moan, she dissolved in his arms. The flame rose higher inside him as he coaxed her full participation in the kiss. She contributed to it, met it equally. Her hands crept over his shoulders. Her fingers tangled in his hair. Tugging his head down, she ran her tongue persistently along his lips.

One taste of Carrie's desire, and Jake sank into the fire. His hands shook as he tugged at the hem of her blouse. He thought he'd never find bare skin, but then his fingers slid beneath the cotton material to caress the length of her spine. He could barely breathe. One hand pressed flat, he moved her slightly. His other hand eased forward, skimming upward over her smooth skin until his knuckles bumped the bottom of one lace-covered breast.

Carrie gasped. "Jake, please!"

Was she begging for his touch or demanding he stop? He couldn't tell. He did know he'd die if she asked him to stop. "Carrie, honey, I have to touch you," he muttered softly into her ear.

"Oh, yes," she moaned, pressed fully into the cradle of his hips.

Carrie's sweet curves, the soft noises she made as she buried into his embrace, drove Jake to the edge. His legs braced wide to steady them both, he cupped the fullness of her breast in his hand. With a sigh of pleasure, he rolled the tender nub of her nipple between his thumb and index finger until it hardened with demand beneath the fragile lace.

Hot need crashed over him. Fast and hard. It overwhelmed his senses until Carrie's touch, her scent, her loving murmur, was his only reality. He nibbled her kiss-swollen mouth, then soothed it with a rough caress of his tongue. When her cool fingertips flipped open the buttons of his shirt and fluttered against his fevered skin, his throaty groan rasped through the night air. Loud. Approving. "Honey," he sucked in a breath when her nail scraped his nipple, "maybe we'd better take this inside."

Her fingers trailed a delicate path over his ribs. She paused to knead, to explore, then traveled on to a new discovery. An eternity later, her lips moved against the hollow at the base of his neck. "What?"

Jake's husky laugh died somewhere in the middle of his chest. "We'll both be facing indecent exposure charges in a few minutes, if we don't take this inside." He had an abysmal lack of control whenever he touched this woman.

Her fingers curled into the hair over his heart. "Sweet mercy," she exclaimed as her face flamed. "I-I don't know why I...you must think...oh, God, I'm sorry!"

He loved the sweet confusion in her eyes. "I'm not," he said, nuzzling the hair at her temple. The action was meant to slow his heartbeat long enough to lead her back into the house where her son slept, to reality. But that one touch wove around his intent and squeezed it into submission. His head lowered for another kiss.

One more. Then, he'd have to let her go.

~~~

A distant alarm impinged on Carrie's mind like a tiny mosquito probing for sustenance. She slapped it away and rose once again to the soaring heights borne of Jake's kiss. Something didn't feel right, but it certainly wasn't Jake. He was heat and passion, hard muscle and bone-deep strength, all wrapped up in mobile lips and a tender touch, oxygen for a starved heart.

The beat of his heart wild against her palm, she blazed an ill-defined path over furred pectoral muscles. It was when her arms slid, unobstructed, around him that she registered what was wrong. His holster hadn't impeded the way.

The unwelcome warning in her head gathered strength and tore her away. "Where's your gun?"

Jake responded to her alarm, but not in any way she

expected. "What's wrong?" With one arm around her shoulders, he dragged her into his side and slightly behind him, his left hand reaching for his gun. Cursing when he came up empty-handed, he scanned the shadows that rimmed the lit yard. "Carrie," he said, "tell me what I'm looking for."

She was alternately repelled and exhilarated by the speed with which he'd come to her defense. More frightened by the array of feelings his actions had awakened than the actions themselves, she tried to pull away. "What are you doing? Let go!"

He held fast. "First, tell me what frightened you."

Her breath caught at the force in his gaze. How had she forgotten the danger this man represented to her peace of mind, to her heart? "You," she blurted. "You frighten me."

As if stung, he released her. "Why?"

Raking her tumbled hair with an unsteady hand, she groped for sanity. "I-It's just that you aren't wearing your gun and I-I...forget it. It doesn't matter."

"The hell it doesn't," he said. "I locked my gun away today because I know it makes you nervous. But it's more than that, isn't it?"

He was so near the truth, she had to put half the yard between them before she could think. Her head spun as she thrust her blouse hem back into her skirt, but she managed to register Jake's approach. "Stop! I don't want you to touch me."

He stopped. "You can't deny what just happened here. You want me as much as I want you."

The acute hunger bubbling through her bloodstream testified to the accuracy of his claim, but she was in no mood to make sense of the emotional mishmash in her brain. With one look, he stirred up needs she hadn't allowed to surface since she was a lonely child in households full of children. With a touch, he dredged up passion she'd thought existed only in books. He reminded her of dreams long forgotten and nightmares she'd never forget.

"I-I can't want you."

"Why not?"

Her lips pursed together. "Because."

"Because? What kind of answer is that? You sound like Eric. I don't have cooties, for God's sake."

It was an effort for her not to smile. Jake and his wounded male ego were hard to withstand. Collapsing on the picnic bench, she rested her head in her hands and whispered. "How did I get involved with anyone, let alone a cop?" She spoke up when her head lifted. "Let's just drop this, Jake. It won't solve anything."

Striding to the table, he straddled the bench facing her. "You're serious. What have you got against cops? We're normal people," he tucked a strand of hair behind her ear, "with normal desires."

It was the desire he provoked inside *her* that concerned her. Unable to sit still, she jumped up to pace the yard. If she told him about Tomás, maybe he'd understand why this insane attraction between them was out of the question. Her resistance was clearly not what she thought it to be, and she needed help to get it back in place. She looked at Jake and blurted, "My husband was killed by a cop."

He jerked as though slapped. "When? What happened?"

Hugging herself to hold the raw emotion at bay, she forced a detachment into her voice. "On March sixteenth six years ago, Tomás went to our bank. There was a bank robber. The police came. When it was all over, there were two dead men. The robber and my husband."

She'd regret until her dying breath that she'd hounded him to go to the bank that day. If she hadn't insisted he ease her mind and talk personally to the loan manager refinancing their home mortgage, Tomás wouldn't have been in the wrong place at the wrong time.

Ironically, his death secured their home irrevocably—the mortgage insurance paid off the house—but she'd lost the most important sanctuary of all, her husband's love. The first love she could call her own.

Jake rose to add his arms to her protective circle. "You were there," he said, more a statement than a question.

"Eric had a cold. I'd gone to the drugstore across the street." She buried her face in the nearest haven, Jake's broad chest, drawing on his solid strength to get through the rest. "It was awful. When I came outside, the bank was surrounded. The next few hours were a nightmare. Some special police eventually entered the bank."

His arms tightened around her. "A S.W.A.T. team."

Her nod didn't keep the images from flooding her head, drowning her in the memories. "They wouldn't let me see Tomás until he was in the...until afterwards." The tears behind her eyelids burned, but she'd cried herself out years ago.

Jake wanted to smash something. He hadn't expected this soul-wrenching bombardment, didn't know how to give Carrie comfort. Cradling her quaking body, he whispered soft assurances in Italian and stroked her hair. He understood now, all too well, why she held him at a distance. Sympathy for her pain and loss, anger at the situation that stood between them, and hopelessness for what he faced if he continued his pursuit of her ripped at his insides.

His team trained hard to avoid situations such as she described. It was a scenario every law officer hoped never to face. What Carrie didn't know was that Jake dealt with it more often than most and, therein, lay the crux of the matter. It was bad enough he wore a police uniform and carried a gun. He was also a card-carrying member of a S.W.A.T. team. Quite likely, the same one that entered her bank that day.

The incident was unfamiliar because the team was drawn from several different precincts and he'd only joined S.W.A.T. a year ago alongside his partner, Ramón. But that wasn't going to matter to Carrie, especially if she learned about the incident with the drug dealer that had prompted his vacation. No. When she found out what he was, she'd bolt so fast his head would spin.

Jake brushed his knuckles over her flushed cheek. "I'm sorry your husband was taken from you, Carrie, but you can't blame all of us for an incident six years in the past."

"I'm sorry, too. I didn't want to dump this all on you." Her eyes filled with unshed tears. "I-I just can't get involved with you."

With three languages at his command, he was at a loss for words. "Honey, I'm more than my job," he said. "I'm like everyone else. I feel pain and joy. I want love and security and happiness." He wanted this woman with an intensity that unsettled him. She had the ability to cut him off at the knees, turn him completely inside out, and he wasn't sure he liked being at her mercy.

"You deserve every bit of that and more." She placed her open palm against his tense jaw. "There's a woman out there who'll fulfill all those dreams." Her hand dropped. "But I can't be that woman. I'm sorry. I'm not interested." She turned and ran into the house.

Minutes later, Jake heard the front door close and a mixture of feminine and childish voices fading down the sidewalk. It was quiet when he sat on the bench again and reached for the tablecloth abandoned in the grass at his feet.

Now what?

Chapter Eight

Jake leaned against the kitchen counter and scraped a chunk of dried wallpaper paste from his T-shirt, his cell jammed between his shoulder and his ear. He shouldn't have answered the phone. His mother's usual catch-up monologue passed through his head unregistered. He had enough on his mind without worrying about whether or not Mama's neighbor's cat had hairballs.

"When's the wedding?"

Damn it. He knew better than to get sidetracked when talking with his mother. "Who's getting married?"

Her sigh was exaggerated. "I knew I shouldn't have left you to your own devices. I thought the whole idea of my returning home was to let you pursue your woman in peace."

Jake winced. Peace had been in short supply these past few days. He'd wasted time cursing, with equal fervor, both his captain and the spare bedroom wallpaper. He'd called Uncle Jules at home the day after the barbecue in the hope he'd reconsider Jake's vacation, allow him to cut it short. After cussing him out for pushing the issue, his uncle had talked about several things unrelated to work and tried again to convince him to join his cousins at Lake Powell.

Ready to tear into something, he'd tackled the wallpaper in the second bedroom only to realize he was doing more harm than good and left it for another day. His biggest frustration? He hadn't seen Carrie since the barbecue on Sunday.

His ear picked up the familiar noise of metal against metal. "What do you have cooking, Mama?"

The snort in his ear was deafening. "Obviously a lot more than you do," she retorted. "What happened to your trip to the mountains today? Weren't you supposed to hike into the wilderness with Brody?"

"I canceled."

"You're getting good at this cancellation business."

He wouldn't have accepted the invitation in the first place if he'd known his fellow officer, Brody Jamison, had an ulterior motive beyond honing his search-and-rescue skills when he'd asked Jake along. His friend neglected to tell him about his plan to dump one of his sisters on Jake while he dallied with a badge bunny of his own. Jake had enough problems.

"You're in trouble already with the widow woman, aren't you?"

He cursed his mother's perceptiveness as Carrie's image wavered in his head. His body hardened with need. Yes. He was in trouble, but some things were best not shared with a man's mother. Still, he wanted to discuss Carrie's revelations with someone who wasn't as invested in the problem. "I guess you could say that."

"Is this the one, Jake?"

The soft question prompted a confused response in his head. *Yes. No. Maybe.* "I don't have a clue what you're talking about, Mama."

Yet, he did know. As irrational as it seemed, he'd

always believed he'd recognize his mate when he saw her—his father claimed to have fallen in love with his mother on sight—but Jake's experience with Daniela had shaken his confidence. He'd sworn to never let his uniform come between him and a woman again. What if he'd found his other half now, only to discover she hated everything for which he stood?

"I watched you together on Sunday. You're different with her. I think this time, this one, you can love."

Mama had conveniently forgotten she had her heart set on Daniela, and that was fine with him. She couldn't be blamed for the way things turned out. He just wished she'd find something else to focus on besides her only son's marital status. It was bad enough before his dad's death, but with Lorenzo Stefani gone, Mama had become obsessed with Jake's lack of bambinos.

He shook his head when Eric's eager expression came to mind and glanced at the tablecloth now folded neatly in the center of his kitchen table. "That's not the issue here."

"She's—" His mother tsked as she did when the English words she wanted didn't immediately come to mind. "What is the saying? *Into* you? Ah, yes! She is into you."

He cringed at her attempt use American slang, but this time she was right. Carrie *was* into him, no matter what she said to the contrary. "She's not into what I do for a living."

A flood of terse Italian burned the airwaves. "What is wrong with your woman? I was proud to be married to a policeman. Police work is in your blood. Papa would turn in his grave to hear such talk."

When the ranting stopped, Jake told her about Carrie's husband.

"That poor woman." She hesitated. "Does she know—"

"There wasn't time." A muttered phrase he refused to translate to English cut him off. "All right. No. Carrie doesn't know about S.W.A.T. She already has problems with my job."

"You have to tell her eventually."

"Maybe. Maybe not. I've been wondering lately if I made the wrong decision."

When the hell had that thought crossed your mind? Coming within inches of death on that last bust must have messed with his head more than he thought.

The heresy scandalized his mother, too. "You weren't wrong to join the S.W.A.T. Papa—"

"Enough! Just because he did it doesn't mean it's right for me." He clamped his lips on the irritation the revelation cost him. He'd held on so tight the last year, he hadn't thought to wonder *why* he was holding on. If he were honest with himself, he'd been questioning a number of his decisions since he'd helped Juanita Reyes bury her youngest child four months ago. He hadn't been able to give her the same closure with her oldest son, Julio.

His mental curse was vivid. This vacation was driving him nuts. There was too much time to think about his chronic restlessness...his career...the kid across the street with no father and hero worship in his eyes, and a luscious woman with too much pain in hers.

He sat in a chair at the table and rubbed a corner of Carrie's tablecloth between two fingers. The material, he decided, wasn't nearly as smooth, as satiny, as his neighbor's fragrant skin. "The point is Carrie has to accept me as a cop before I spring anything else on her." She also had to give him another shot at changing her perceptions.

"I hope you know what you're doing."

So did he. There were those who'd advise him, at this point, to give up. To accept that his stubborn, relentless pursuit of what was probably a lost cause, was a waste of time and effort. Those people hadn't met Carrie. It might take a miracle, but before he was through his captivating neighbor would come to terms with his occupation.

With any luck, there wouldn't be time over the last two-and-a-half weeks of his vacation to delve any further into his troublesome questions about his career.

~~~

Carrie sat on her bed with the list of chores she'd jotted down over coffee yesterday. *This isn't working.* The last few days when she wasn't busy at the office, she'd been a frenetic little bee at home. She'd accomplished wonders with the dust bunnies under the furniture, a five-course meal could be served on literally every surface in the house, and the linen closet and Eric's sock and underwear drawers had never looked better.

Jake still refused be cleansed from her mind.

The sound of Eric and Davy playing catch in the front yard faded from her hearing as she once again itemized her reasons for avoiding Jake. It just wouldn't work out. Her fears were too deeply embedded. She wasn't in danger from a mind-blowing desire for him. His eyes weren't nearly as sensitive and caring as she'd made them out to be, and she didn't feel that much more alive when he was around.

Yeah, right. There was an ache in her chest that grew with each passing day and her body seemed stuck in yearn mode. She'd repeatedly checked Jake's house since Sunday, but he was noticeably absent from view. She didn't know what bothered her more, not catching one glimpse of the man she'd rejected or her growing need to see him.

In less than a week, she'd become a walking, talking basket case. Her concentration was shot, especially at work. Sam hadn't said anything yet, but it was only a matter of time. Many more days like the last two and she might as well kiss her shot at the new Berthoud office good-bye.

Friend or not, Sam couldn't afford the kind of mistakes she was making. Despite his reassurances, she knew he wasn't happy with the way she'd handled an irate client this afternoon. It wasn't her only misstep, but definitely the worst since it looked like O'Reilly Realty had lost the man's lucrative account. It wasn't her fault the client made demands she couldn't fulfill but she hadn't handled it as well as she might have if her mind had been on business instead of Jake.

So, where did that leave her? With terrible longings she couldn't satisfy, feelings that shouldn't even matter, or the opportunity to be with a man who singed her insides? She glared at her reflection in the mirror across the room. The answer should be simple, yet it wasn't. It was a good thing the decision was out of her hands. She'd seen to that after Jake's barbecue, hadn't she?

Downstairs, the front door slammed. "Mooom," Eric yelled from the foyer. "Where are you?"

Carrie stood and smoothed her jean shorts. She

made a face in the mirror, pushing a stray hair back into her braid. "Here, Eric," she called. Walking out of her bedroom, she headed for the top of the stairs.

Eric beamed up at her. "Jake's here."

Shocked to see the very man she was obsessing about standing at the bottom of her staircase, she froze. For the first time since Sunday, excitement blasted through her veins and swept away the sickness in her heart. So much for any delusions of closure!

Her gaze lingered on the black T-shirt molding Jake's muscular chest, the jeans that hugged his hips, down strong legs to tennis shoes with one shoelace too loosely tied. He was undeniably the sexiest, most appealing, man she'd ever met. But it was his smile that folded around her heart.

Recovering her balance with difficulty, she walked slowly down the stairs until she was at eye level with his gaze. "Hi," she said, mentally cursing her breathlessness. She looked at his mouth, then away to his eyes again.

Big mistake. Even his eyes were smiling at her.

"Bye, Mom," Eric said from the doorway. "I'm running with Davy to his house to get his new bat. Jake said he'd throw some balls for us."

The boys were gone before she could gather her wits, leaving her alone with the man she'd missed entirely too much.

"They'll only be gone a few minutes," Jake said quietly. "We need to talk."

She moistened her dry lips. "I guess we do."

He stared at her mouth. His shoulders rolled slightly as if there was an itch he couldn't quite reach. Then he drew himself up, a restive look on his face.

"Despite my good intentions, we're going to settle something first," he said before dragging her down one more stair into his arms. Her hands settled onto his shoulders seconds before he kissed her.

His lips were soft and coaxing, hard and demanding. Dizziness settled over Carrie's mind as the sensations won through to obliterate thought. Jake was here, holding her tight, and she felt alive again. Nourished, as never before. Her moan of surrender was trapped in his mouth.

His lips brushed over hers in long, slow movements sipping her like expensive brandy. She broke away with a gasp and buried her face in his neck. Everything about him was strong, secure. She longed to place her shivery skin against his, to wrap herself in his heat so she'd never be cold again.

One of his hands cupped the back of her head. He tugged gently on her braid, all the while murmuring something in Italian. She didn't know what he was saying, but just the raw tone made her insides melt.

He tilted her face up for another hungry, seeking kiss. Carrie knew the danger of jumping into the deep end without knowing how to swim, but she took on every bit of his desire and silently asked for more. Jake would keep her safe. He'd be her lifeline.

He denied her the satisfaction she craved. His head lifted. "Now tell me you're not interested," he said roughly.

How could she argue the point with such incontrovertible evidence to the contrary? "I-I can't."

A smile tugged at his lips. "Good. Then we work from here."

"But—"

"Shh. Just give this a little time."

Carrie rubbed shaky hands on her legs. She wanted to believe it was that simple, that an entire lifetime of heartache and loss could be erased with a snap of fingers. She'd given up on that illusion long ago. "Time won't make a difference."

Jake stepped back, giving her more breathing room. "I've less than three weeks of vacation left. Give me that. You control where we go from here. I won't even try to kiss you again, unless you flat out ask me to." His eyes darkened with intent. "If you still feel the same way when I go back to work, I'll leave you alone. I won't bother you again."

"You expect me to forget what you do?"

He remained still, watchful. "Until I return to work, I'm not a cop. You're not a real estate agent. We're just two people getting to know each other."

"You're asking too much."

A deep line creased his brow. "Where does that leave us? As neighbors, acquaintances? What?"

Carrie ached with regret. Why did this hurt so much? "It's true there's something between us, Jake, but it's physical. It'll pass. The most we'll ever be is friends. Nothing more."

"Friends." It sounded like a curse when he said it.

He studied her. Whether to give himself time to come up with arguments or to gauge her resolve, Carrie didn't know. Then he smiled. It was a wicked smile, one that made her wish she hadn't drawn such distinct lines over which neither of them could cross. His eyes promised everything, daring her to deny she wanted anything.

"Okay, honey," he said, "we'll do this your way.

You convince me we'll never be anything but friends. I'll make you see otherwise. Deal?"

What kind of deal is that?

His head cocked arrogantly when she remained silent. "You're scared. You know friends don't spark against each other the way we do. That scares you to death."

"Don't be ridiculous." She could be as strong as she needed to be. Maybe. "No more kissing?"

"No kissing." He grinned. "Unless you beg me."

Her heart skipped a beat at the delicious thought of begging him for one of his shattering kisses, of getting it just because she'd demanded it. "I can't believe you have me negotiating like this. You're the most stubborn, exasperating—"

He placed his index finger over her lips. "So I have two little character flaws. Sue me. I won't take no for an answer."

Her mouth tingled beneath the light touch. It took all of her willpower to not purse her lips and kiss the ridges on his fingertip. That would lead to a taste, which would lead to...

Sweet mercy, her willpower was proving shallow at best when it came to this man. "Well, I'm not going to simply say yes either."

"Then, I guess we understand each other."

Nonplussed, she stared at his confident expression. Sooner or later, Jake would have to accept defeat. Once they got past all the physical stuff, they'd settle into a friendly relationship like she had with Sam. It might be boring, but safe. All the same, she wished she didn't feel as though she'd thrown away something of value.

"Um." She cleared her throat. "Is that all you

wanted? I mean, was there another reason why you came over?"

He gestured at the swath of cloth resting on the entry table behind him. "You forgot your tablecloth on Sunday."

No. She'd dropped everything and run away like her panties were on fire. "Thanks."

They stared at each other. Jake appeared prepared to stay right where he was all day, but Carrie didn't think there was anything more to do or say. Another mind-blowing kiss was out of the question. She'd cut off any possibility of that ever happening again."

"Are you in the mood for pizza?"

The question was the last thing she expected. "Pizza?"

He nodded. "Eric mentioned a craving for pizza, and dinner sounds great to me. I'm hungry. Aren't you?"

She was starving. But, it would probably be safer to concentrate on a hunger she could actually appease. "If you're talking all meat, with extra cheese and onions, I can put away my share."

Jake grinned. "Mmm. My kind of woman." He headed for the door, then glanced over his shoulder. "I'll be back in about an hour with Eric. It's all right if I take him to the park a couple of blocks over, isn't it? I did promise to give him and Davy some batting pointers."

She nodded, feeling lighter in spirit than she'd felt in ages. "Go ahead. It will give me time to change."

~~~

Two hours later, Carrie sat next to her son in an upholstered, red-checked booth, a hot, gooey pizza sitting on the table in front of them. While Eric gave Jake a play-by-play description of his last baseball game, she surreptitiously watched the man she bumped knees with beneath the small table. What was it about Jake that made her tear down the emotional walls she'd worked so hard to build, with little thought and few questions asked?

She watched his lips move as he ate. She examined the way his yellow cotton, button-down shirt accentuated his dark, good looks, then admired the way it stretched across his wide chest as he reached for another slice of pizza. Her pulse skipped a beat. She'd have to be catatonic, not to be affected by this man.

But when he teased Eric into another giggle, it was all too easy to see why she was having such a hard time turning her back on Jake. There was a lot more to the man beyond his ability to melt her insides. He truly cared about the people around him, an appealing trait the neglected child within her could appreciate.

He talked to Eric, not at him. He listened to what her son had to say. Then his hand ruffled Eric's hair when he said something pleasing. In less than twenty minutes, her eight-year-old had shared secrets with Jake of which she knew nothing. Eric hadn't told *her* he had a crush on his second grade math teacher. No wonder his math scores had improved so much this year!

She was ashamed to admit it, but a twinge of jealousy tugged at her heart. Too busy pushing Jake away, she'd missed the connection the two males had forged. It was a bit daunting to realize Eric was that easily bowled over by a few throws of a ball in the park and a sloppy pizza on a plastic plate. He'd been more desperate for male companionship than she'd suspected.

It only took a few kisses and the same sloppy pizza to get you here, a voice chided in her head. *What is it that you're desperate for?*

She thrust the question away, unaware Jake had spoken to her until Eric poked her ribs with his elbow. Caught with a slice of pizza in her mouth, she focused on Jake's inquisitive expression.

Her confusion must have showed. "I wondered if you had any objections," he said.

Swallowing the chunk of pizza she'd bitten off without chewing it, she choked and dabbed at her face with a napkin to catch a hot glob of runaway cheese.

Jake reached over to swipe a callused finger over her mouth. Then, he glanced at Eric. "Does your mom always eat that way?"

Eric giggled. "Sometimes it's worse. You should see her eat corn-on-the-cob."

She gave in to self-conscious laughter. "Can I help it if I love my corn dripping in butter?"

"I'm interested in learning about all the things you love," Jake murmured. His gaze clashed with hers for long poignant seconds that made her heart beat faster before he clarified his earlier question. "Would you mind if I tagged along Saturday and watched Eric's games? If I'm going to be his batting coach, I need a better idea of what he's doing."

One look down at her son's hopeful expression, and Carrie knew she was licked. How could she object when Eric deserved all of the personal attention Jake was willing to give him? She couldn't hurt her son by limiting his contact with the man.

The question was how was she going to limit her contact with Jake? Saying she had the strength to resist him was one thing. Testing that spirit over and over again might prove to be another. "Sure. Come along," she said. "We have to be at the ballpark by nine."

Chapter Nine

Jake hoped Saturday's cloudless sky was a sign that he, too, would soon see his way clear to a certain woman's heart. He'd maneuvered an invitation to Eric's baseball game today, but accomplished little else in his bid for entry into Carrie's life. Since the night at the pizza parlor, Jake had spoken to her several times, but those conversations were brief and took place on the sidewalk outside her house when she was on the way somewhere. He couldn't decide if her schedule was truly that full or she was avoiding him.

Eric, on the other hand, spent every spare second after school trailing Jake, often with Davy or another neighborhood friend in tow. Jake hadn't realized how limited his contact had become with kids whose only thoughts were of the next ball game or which cute girl sat next to them in class. The youthful company and his new status as a neighborhood hero were oddly satisfying.

If only Carrie would look at him as if he were the answer to all her prayers, Jake could be a happy man. If he didn't have the memory of three incredible, scorching kisses to cling to—

A disgruntled voice broke through his musing. "What did I do wrong this time, Jake?"

He leaned into the chain link fence and looked at Eric, slouched on the bullpen bench. Jake had missed the last strike, but the first two swings were vivid enough in his mind. "You're stepping into the swing too early."

"Last time you said I was too late," the boy grumbled. "It felt the same to me."

Jake chuckled. "When you do it right, you'll know the difference. Watch the ball, not the pitcher. Don't let him pull your timing off. With practice and patience, you'll get it."

A sound piece of advice, he decided, rubbing at an ache lodged in his temple. He ought to listen to his own counsel. Patience wasn't any easier for him, though, not when he wanted something badly enough. A couple of hours alone with Carrie, preferably with a lock between them and the world, and Jake would settle this friends versus lovers business once and for all.

His experience with Daniela notwithstanding, he knew he wanted Carrie in his bed. Whether his enticing neighbor would fit into his life was another question to be answered with time, a premium within the limits of his vacation. With two weeks to win Carrie over, patience threatened to fall off his list of priorities.

He'd been frustrated on all fronts lately. He'd had no luck locating Julio Reyes either. Jake checked on the kid's mother, something he'd done once a month since Mateo's death, but he could tell by her crushed manner that she'd lost hope of ever hearing from her older son. Several forays through known SKL territory hadn't turned up anything on the missing gangbanger either. According to Jake's snitches, even the Dragons had gone to ground since the last drug bust carved a big chunk out of their organization. Ramón wasn't having any better luck. It looked more and more like Julio had been eliminated and it was only a matter of time before someone found his body.

Which left Jake wrestling with the one problem he should be able to solve. *Carrie.*

He searched the bleachers behind the backstop at home plate where she'd been sitting the last dozen times he'd looked. She wasn't there. His eyes narrowed against the harsh noon sunlight, he searched the ball field until he spotted her on the grass strip under a stand of cottonwoods that ran alongside the first base sideline. She and another team mother were setting up a meal at a pair of picnic tables where Eric's team would eat between games.

Jake's stomach rumbled at the thought of lunch — he'd skipped breakfast to meet with Ramón before picking up his neighbors — but it was Carrie, in bare feet and a poppy-strewn halter dress that really got his juices flowing. The matching scarf holding her ponytail topped off the image of a gaily-wrapped present and simply begged for removal. He could think of nothing that would finish off his day — and night — better than unwrapping her in the privacy of his bedroom.

When he turned his gaze back to Eric, he realized the boy was still looking to him for pearls of baseball wisdom. "You'll get it," he assured him. "Look for your opportunity. Then, jump on it with everything you've got."

Personally, he wondered if Eric, or himself, for that matter, would ever get past first base.

~~~

When Eric hit a home run in the last inning, Carrie couldn't tell who was more surprised, Jake or Eric. She did know who was the most excited.

"Did you see it, Mom?" Eric wedged his body into his seat at the picnic table, oblivious to the fact his wiggling dislodged Todd Perkins, the shortstop, from his precarious perch at the other end. "It went over the fence." His arm arced in demonstration, knocking another teammate's hat off his head. "Clean over, Mom!"

Carrie smiled, picked Todd off the ground with one hand and plucked the hat out of the potato chip bowl with the other. "I saw it, kiddo. You really whacked it."

He beamed at her then at his friends, still chattering a mile a minute. His team lost their first game, but it didn't matter. Eric had finally hit a ball, and it was all thanks to the neighbor who stubbornly refused to stay out of her thoughts by day and her dreams by night.

She wasn't dealing particularly well with her own personal demons, but Eric had gained a wealth of confidence in as many short days. "Thank you," she said to Jake. "You made his week."

He shrugged away her praise. "He did it, not me."

The door to her heart opened another crack. She'd seen Jake's crossed fingers when Eric was three-and-two at home plate. "It was more than I could do."

Her hand rested on his forearm. The impulsive touch sabotaged the tight control she enveloped herself in whenever Jake was near. The feel of hot skin beneath her palm reminded her of one of her most lurid nightly fantasies. One which included stripping off his police uniform, one piece at a time, dragging her fingers through the soft hair on his muscular chest, and —

A shiver of alarm shattered the fantasy. *Uniform?* Since when did Jake wear his uniform in her dreams? As if scalded, her hand jerked back. "I-I appreciate the time," she stammered, "you've given Eric."

"We still have a lot of work to do, though, don't we?" he cautioned. His knuckles brushed the length of her jaw. His fingers tangled in her ponytail and remained there, leisurely massaging her scalp. When her scarf came undone, her hair tumbled with wild abandon around her face.

With one smooth movement, Jake tucked the scarf into his jeans pocket and finger-combed her hair away from her temple like he had all day to just touch her. "Just because Eric hit the ball once doesn't mean he'll hit it every time."

He was still talking about baseball, right? "He'll get it right more often now that you've given him pointers," she said, desperate to hold on to a thread of the conversation, an impossible task under his intimate ministrations. "That's what's important."

Sweet mercy! When had her scalp become an erogenous zone?

Each gentle tug of his fingers reached deeper inside her until every last nerve ending tingled down to her bare toes. With each touch, he retraced the line she'd sketched between them. With one intent look, he challenged her from his side of the line. She was tempted, again and again, to cross into territory she knew to be dangerous.

Caught by the lure of Jake's confident smile, she didn't immediately recognize the benefits of the silence that had fallen between them. Pulling her scattered wits together, she moved away to the second picnic table where another team mother helped her to serve up lunch to nine hungry ball players.

They ladled chili over franks, dug for missing plastic forks, and chased after windblown napkins and paper cups. It was after Carrie waved the other woman off to her nursing shift with the promise to give her son's inhaler to her husband when he arrived that she finally stopped to take a breath.

That's when Jake caught up with her. "This is great." His arm settled naturally around her shoulders. "Who dreamed up this idea of a picnic lunch for everyone?"

She was too conscious of the way his hand curved over her arm, preventing her escape should she want one. The further hint of surrender to her misbehaving hormones stiffened her backbone. Draping herself all over Jake in a fantasy was one thing, but her traitorous body wasn't allowed to mold itself to him in broad daylight as well!

Her gaze fixed on the kids eating their meal several feet away. "One day after practice," she explained, "a team mother set out a picnic lunch for her family. Before she knew it, all the kids had begged fried chicken from her. It was such a hit, we decided one lunch for everyone made sense, even for those days when there's only one game.

"We take turns so no one's overworked, while making sure that none of the kids go hungry on game day." She regarded her son. "I like doing this for Eric."

Jake nodded approvingly. "It shows your love and support and brings the two of you together. He knows he has a prominent place in your heart, no matter how busy you are."

Carrie didn't need the reminder of how busy her schedule had been lately. "A child needs to know he's loved."

"That sounds like experience talking."

The observation hit one of the never-quite-healed bruises on her battered heart. "Experience is a great teacher."

"You didn't feel loved by your parents?"

"No," she admitted, "but a child's impressions aren't always the right ones." She shrugged. "My parents split up when I was Eric's age. Dad followed his engineering job to South America. Mom married a man who didn't want kids. They both loved me, but Dad couldn't take a child with him and Mom wasn't capable of caring for herself, let alone me. Shortly after she remarried, Mom was diagnosed with her first bout of cancer."

"Which left you where?"

"Confused. Frightened. Bouncing between relatives. I was a senior in high school before I accepted that my parents had done their best. But, by then, I'd grown up feeling more of a burden than anything else."

Jake scowled. "Your dad should've come back and taken you with him, not allowed you to be pawned off where you didn't feel welcome."

She felt comforted by his anger on her behalf. "His work took him to remote locations that, more often than not, were unsafe. By the time mom died, I was able to take care of myself."

"How often do you see him now?"

His thunderous expression told her not to share that her father's last visit to the States had been when he brought his Colombian wife—and the teenage son he'd raised in the same unsafe environment—to meet her. Eric was two months old at the time, so the visit wasn't nearly as painful as she'd expected. "He pops in whatever he can but we communicate mostly through email."

Turning away from family dynamics she couldn't change, she nodded at her son. "Anyway, the instant I looked into Eric's sweet, innocent face, I vowed he would always know how much I cared, how much he means to me."

"You've done a good job." Jake gestured toward the over-crowded picnic table. "Look at him. He's one happy little boy now."

What she saw was that Eric had yet to come down from his high over his home run. "You had more to do with that than me." Her son had always looked to her for everything he needed. Until Jake came along. "Eric thinks you're Superman."

Jake ducked his head, clearly embarrassed if the bright flags of color in his face were any indication. "I just gave him a few pointers."

"Why?" The question had niggled at her for days.

"Why what?"

"Why spend hours with a child that you barely know teaching him to hit a ball?"

Lost in thought much longer than the question warranted, Jake finally spoke. "Eric reminds me of a ten-year-old boy I once knew. More than that, he's a reminder of a vow I made." A frown creased his forehead. "Mateo Reyes lived in the apartment complex where I used to live. He didn't have a dad, so he looked up to me like a big brother. He had a sixteen-year-old brother, but he was gone a lot so Mateo dogged my footsteps for months."

"What happened?"

"Mateo followed in his brother's footsteps and joined his gang. He was killed two weeks later because his brother angered the gang leader."

Carrie gasped at the pain in Jake's eyes. "And the brother?"

"We can't find him."

The resignation in his voice, in his expression, told her a lot. "You think he suffered the same fate."

"It's possible."

She placed a comforting hand over Jake's heart. "You blame yourself." If she'd learned nothing else about the man, she knew his protective instincts were such an integral part of him that failure would strike deep into his soul.

"The morning Mateo died," he said, "he came to me for help. I'd been working on him to leave the gang, but my relationship with Daniela had imploded so I told him to come back later that day." He stirred restlessly and threaded his fingers through hers to pull her into him. When their bodies were completely aligned, he continued. "I found him in the alley behind our building that night. He was gone before I could get him help."

Carrie's heart ached for the little boy who would never grow up and for the man who felt responsible. "You couldn't have known what would happen."

"I'm a cop, honey. I knew. Mateo's dead because I didn't listen when he needed me."

Her fingers tightened around his. "And your vow?"

"I'm going to wipe out the gang who killed him. I won't turn my back on a kid in need again."

She appreciated the insight into Jake's job, into what motivated him both as a man and a cop. But her heart faltered at the thought that suddenly popped into her head. "Do you think Eric's a kid in need, like Mateo?"

"If you're asking if he's in immediate danger of joining a gang, my answer is no, he's not. I meant to tell you that I checked with his school officer. The initiation that got him and Davy into trouble wasn't about joining a gang. The kids were intrigued with the idea of hanging with some sixth graders that play ball together, of having a bunch of big brothers." He smiled gently. "He has you, and now he has me to keep him on the straight and narrow. All he really needed was someone to teach him how to hit a ball."

Relief swamped through her. "Eric might think of you as *his* hero, but you're mine, too." Raising her head, she kissed Jake's hard jaw. "I've been so worried. Thank you for setting my mind at rest."

He grinned wickedly at her. "If I'd known a kiss was my reward, I might have worked faster."

Carrie laughed self-consciously at the reminder there wasn't supposed to be any kissing going on between them. She looked around for a distraction. Grabbing the pot of chili, she crossed to the team table and began refilling plates with the leftovers. Jake handed out cupcakes. By the time she shooed the kids off to the ball field and started cleaning up, she was humming under her breath.

"I think these lunches are as fun for you as they are for Eric," Jake said with a laugh, pulling her down to the picnic bench beside him. "How often do you do it?"

"Not often enough," she said, watching the team coach give the boys instructions before their next game. "I work most weekends."

"Why? You'd rather be here."

She shrugged. "It's part of my job."

Jake looked like he'd just learned her boss ran a chain gang, his face flushed, a frown pulling at his forehead. "I can't believe Sam makes you work that hard."

"I work weekends because that's when people want to look at houses. I need the commissions," she said. "As much as I'd love to spend all my time with Eric, I can't forget my other responsibilities to him. He needs clothes, equipment, all sorts of things.

"What happens when he wants to go to college? Gets married? I have to be prepared for anything." She wasn't likely to forget his happiness sat squarely on her shoulders.

"He'll want all those things eventually, honey," Jake motioned to where Eric had moved into left field, "but he isn't suffering from any immediate lacks I can see."

Watching her son stretch his hamstrings, she knew of at least two. A father and the guidance only a father could provide. She'd proven inadequate to that particular task. Eric's fleeting foray into crime was a direct result of her inattention to what he was doing, but, darn it, she couldn't bulldog his every step. He already spent too much time sitting around her office on weekends.

She pursed her lips. "He won't suffer anything if I can help it. Once I get the job in Berthoud —"

"What job?"

Carrie wasn't prepared for Jake's sharp tone. Neither was she used to explaining her actions. Finding herself on treacherous ground, she stood and busied her hands with the construction of a chili dog for herself. "Sam's building another office in Berthoud," she said, her head lowered over her task. "I intend to manage it."

"You're moving?"

She twisted around fully, unsure why she felt so uneasy when she found Jake standing so near. Her imagination provided a picture of herself challenging a starved mountain lion, a T-bone in her back pocket. "I'm not going anywhere."

"Won't it be hard to live in Riverton and work in Berthoud?"

"Maybe. But I can't afford to buy another house," she said. "It's only a thirty minute commute."

"I know, but—"

Carrie fidgeted under his silent contemplation. "What are we talking about here?"

"Chances. I don't like the thought of you and Eric moving so far away."

It shouldn't matter that he didn't want her to move, but it did. "Afraid you'll have to go out and make all new friends, huh?"

He grinned. "Terrified."

Laughter bubbled inside her. "Liar."

Jake cocked his head to one side, his gaze fixed on her face. "Maybe I'm just feeling neglected."

"You? Neglected? Who would dare?"

He leaned far enough for her to bask in the heat emanating from his body. "You do," he whispered, "all the time. It's driving me out of my mind."

Carrie forgot they were in a public park, in the bright light of day, in the company of two Little League baseball teams and their parents. There was only Jake, herself, and a double truckload of unfulfilled desire. She swallowed. "What do you think I should do about it?"

Jake's eyebrows rose, as if he hadn't expected the throaty quality of her question. Then, the naughty gleam in his eyes intensified. "Well, for a start, you might feed me. Do you know I'm the only one here without a chili dog?"

He wanted food?

She stifled a groan of self-disgust. Jake would never accept friendship as her only desire if she couldn't keep up the pretense with herself. "Take mine," she said, thrusting her plate into his hands. "I'm not hungry, anyway."

Watching him round the table in search of condiments, her scarf peeking from his pocket, her plate balanced on his large hand, she wondered if her accessories and lunch were the only things Jake would walk away with before he was done. It was disconcerting to know that, just for a microsecond, she'd been about to offer him dessert, too.

You're out of cupcakes, a naughty voice whispered in her head. *What will you give him instead?*

Heaven help her, but she was in serious trouble.

~~~

"I bet you poisoned him, Mom," Eric said from the passenger seat of Jake's Mustang later that afternoon.

"Eric," Carrie exclaimed, "don't even think it."

Hands tight on the unfamiliar steering wheel she peered in the rearview mirror at the gray-faced man who half reclined in the back seat. Jake's eyes were shut now but they'd been glazed five minutes ago when she'd poured him into the car at the ball park. Beads of sweat rimmed his upper lip, his forehead.

Poison? Nausea raced through her stomach as quickly as the thought. It was a possibility. She'd never seen a man get ill so fast. Jake literally folded as Eric's second game finished.

What did a person get for poisoning a police officer? Ten years? Twenty? Heaven help her, between coaches, umpires, and the parents at least twenty people ate her chili dogs this afternoon. They'd put her away for life, throw away the key. She'd never see Jake and Eric again.

"Eric, stop scaring your mother. It's flu."

Jake's quiet admonishment over her right shoulder went a long way toward easing her panic. She examined his feverish eyes in the mirror, her worry not as easy to subdue. Her lower lip caught in her teeth, she steered the car to the side of the road and stopped. "Maybe he's right, Jake," she said, flipping on the turn signal. "We'll go to the hospital. If it's poison, they'll have to pump your stomach or something."

"Carrie."

In the rearview mirror, she saw Jake shiver before she checked the street for traffic for her U-turn. "What?"

Jake's fingers pressed into her shoulder until she looked back at him. "It's the flu," he said. "I swear."

His face swam in front of her eyes. She fought the urge to cry. "Are you sure?"

He rested back against the seat. "I'm positive. Food poisoning isn't selective. No one else has any symptoms."

"Maybe you're the first."

He shook his head, then winced. "No. The headache started this morning, and I thought the hollow feeling in my stomach was hunger. Guess I was wrong."

Eric looked around the edge of his bucket seat. "Tony had the flu last week, remember? He thought his head would blow up, it hurt so bad. Wait 'till I tell him you got it, too."

"Next time he comes over with you and Davy, we'll

exchange horror stories," Jake said, ending the conversation. He addressed Carrie. "In the meantime, honey, can you just take us home? No side trips to the hospital."

He didn't have to ask twice. Carrie soon had the car parked in Jake's driveway and the man tucked into his bed. He fell asleep before he finished the cup of peppermint tea she brewed to settle his stomach despite his protests he could take care of himself. It wasn't until she'd tucked a light blanket around his shivering form that she faced facts. Leaving him to fend for himself was not an option. Not after all he'd done for her, for Eric.

She told herself it was simple worry about a friend that prompted her concern, but there was a niggling doubt poking at the backside of her explanation. She'd never felt this driving need to cuddle Joan or Sam to her breast!

~~~

Carrie identified the heavy, thumping sounds above her head before her eyes opened. Someone was stumbling around upstairs. Again.

She came fully awake—the fourth time that night— and toppled off her makeshift bed on Jake's loveseat. In the dim light from the three-way lamp in the corner, she glared at the mass of overstuffed pillows she'd tried to ride since ten o'clock. "For heaven's sake, Mama," she whispered fiercely, "couldn't you have given the man a normal sofa?"

Still muttering, she separated her legs from the tangle of cushions and sheets, and made her way upstairs. She bypassed the first bedroom that Jake had turned into an exercise room, as well as the second. Poking her head into the third room, she identified the lone naked foot sticking out from Eric's sleeping bag on the floor. Her son was a burrower and almost invisible in his flat spread-eagle position, but she was used to discerning his form.

Moving on to the last bedroom, she stopped when she saw the light from the master bath shining onto the empty king-sized bed. She sighed. Jake would never get better at this rate. "There must be a way to keep the man in bed," she muttered.

She rapped on the half-open bathroom door, then looked inside when she got no response. No luck. Her socks whispered against the carpet as she moved back toward the hall. When Jake suddenly appeared before her, she gasped. "You scared me," she exclaimed, one hand pressed to her galloping heart. "Where'd you come from?"

"Sorry," he said, frowning down at her. "I thought there were more blankets in the front room closet. There aren't any there." Like that explanation had used the last of his energy reserves, he propped one shoulder against the doorjamb, his arms limp at his sides. "I'm cold."

"I'm not surprised. I could have sworn you had on pajamas earlier." She stared at a tantalizing amount of bare skin, all goose bumped. He looked so pathetic and so kissable at the same time, her impulse to yell at the man died a small death.

He grimaced. "They're scratchy. I don't usually wear anything."

Carrie hid a smile at his grumpy tone and reveled in the mental image of Jake wearing nothing but his provocative come-and-get-me grin. "Well, thanks for putting on something."

She eyed his sweat pants hugged low on his hips,

outlining every masculine line, especially the bulge that grew under her watchful gaze. Startled, she glanced up into Jake's glazed eyes. *For God's sake, the man can barely stand, let alone do what you're thinking.*

Strangling a moan of self-denial, she turned away and walked back to the middle of the room to lift the discarded bedding off the floor. Jake didn't move even after she'd remade the bed. He'd worn himself out looking for blankets. Why hadn't he asked her to help him?

The man was too darned stubborn for his own good. As sick as he was, he was determined to not yield to his illness. That strength of purpose was a likely asset for a cop, but it was giving Carrie fits. Getting around a recalcitrant Jake was not as easy as getting around a cranky eight-year-old boy.

Or was it?

She suppressed a smile, then scooped up and began to fold Jake's wadded pajamas. "So you hate pajamas," she said conversationally. "That means someone gave these to you. I wonder who sees you as the cupid type?" She examined the material with a critical eye. "The gold arrows shooting through the red hearts are a cute touch, but who—"

Jake growled. "Just help me get to the damned bed, Carrie."

She peered at him over the upturned collar, her eyes wide with innocence. "You want my help?"

"No." His glare wasn't completely successful. "But since you're going to all this trouble to divert me, I might as well let you have your way."

"I like the idea of having my own way for a change."

His eyes danced behind the blur of fever. "Give it

your best shot. I'm in your hands."

Her mouth dropped open. Well, didn't that just conjure up some notions? *Your libido deserves an ice water dip.*

Catching her lower lip between her teeth, she ordered her mind and body to behave. She threw the pajamas toward a chair, walked across the room, and clasped an arm around Jake's waist to help him back to bed. It wasn't until the sheet and blanket was pulled to his chin that she dared to breathe again. "Is that better?"

A violent tremor shook his body. "Still cold," he said in a rush.

She placed her hand against his forehead to confirm what she'd discovered when her arm touched his naked waist. The man was burning up. "Jake, where else can I look for your missing blankets?"

"No clue," he bit out between chattering teeth. "Probably still in a box in the garage."

Her heart ached. She was incredibly anxious about a man she hadn't known very long, but there was little time to consider the ramifications of such a strong emotion. It was the middle of the night, and Jake needed her. She refused to desert him. Tomorrow was soon enough to deal with the consequences of her next actions.

She gave him a couple of pills for his fever, then told him to turn on his side away from her. When he complied with her instruction, she lifted the blanket and slid under it.

"What the—" He tried to roll over, but he was effectively trapped under the sheet she was lying on.

Carrie draped her arm over his waist, spooning herself along the length of his back. "Shh, Jake. You're chilled because of the fever," she explained. "I'll just stay here until the pills kick in and you go to sleep."

A brief silence greeted the resolution in her voice. "At least get under the sheet, too, so you don't get cold," he muttered.

It was a good thing Jake's back was to her. Enough light shone from the bathroom to highlight her smile of triumph, and she didn't want any more arguments from him. "I'm fine," she told him. "I'll go back to my bed in a few minutes."

"You should go home." The words weren't decisive enough to mask his exhaustion.

"For the last time, Jake, I'm staying," she declared. "I know you think you're perfectly capable of taking care of yourself, but you need me."

"You noticed." He looked over his shoulder, a lazy smile playing with his lips. "It's about time."

Carrie searched his glazed eyes and frowned, reminding herself that coherence couldn't be expected from a feverish man. "Shut up, Jake, and go to sleep. For a man in your weakened condition, you sure talk a lot."

Jake yawned, then chuckled sleepily when he was shaken by another shiver. "If I thought I was up to it, I'd argue that point," he settled his head on his pillow, "but, I can wait 'til morning."

Deep, steady breathing a few minutes later confirmed he'd fallen asleep. Still, Carrie didn't move. She'd convinced herself she could hold Jake in her arms for ten minutes without dire consequences. When her eyelids fluttered down, she had two minutes left.

Chapter Ten

Jake renamed Eric's friend, Tony Patterson, 'Typhoid Tony' late Sunday when Eric also came down with the flu. Far from well himself, Jake nevertheless summoned the energy to urge Carrie to use his house as an infirmary for them both.

She returned to work on Tuesday when he claimed to be on the mend, but it was three days before he fully recovered. He cared for Eric during the day, while Carrie babied them both at night after work. Jake lost vacation time, while Eric missed out on the last of his school year. Jake didn't have one complaint.

His illness had accomplished one thing. The wall between him and Carrie was seriously compromised, if not destroyed. He'd awakened Sunday knowing she'd spent the night in his arms, but said nothing to put her on the defensive.

She wouldn't like knowing, in the innocence of sleep, she'd betrayed herself. Drifting awake at dawn he became aware of her, nuzzling his shoulder and neck, her hand pressed protectively over his heart. When his movements disturbed her, she mumbled something indistinct against his throat, while her fingers brushed gently over his skin.

Her unconscious actions were those of a woman

145

concerned for a loved one, and he was damned if he wasn't surprised he liked the fuss. Besides Mama, no one had ever cared for him when he was ill. No woman since had possessed the genuine affection his neighbor seemed to have in abundance.

Jake had tucked her into his side, his eyes closing in contentment despite the familiar discomfort of the erection he woke with each morning since meeting Carrie. He wasn't willing to jeopardize their relationship for a quick tumble in bed. He was holding out for something more permanent.

By the time Eric was healthy again, Jake talked Carrie into allowing the boy to spend the balance of his vacation with him. She'd hired a sitter until Eric went to Florida to visit his father's parents. He wasn't happy with the arrangement, and Jake took blatant advantage of the opportunity to build on his new rapport with both mother and son.

Every morning, Carrie dropped Eric at his front door. After a couple of days, she stayed long enough to share a glass of sweet ice tea with him while Eric finished a movie he was watching on the DVD player. When Jake started preparing dinner for three, she didn't protest. Maybe because the first time he'd done it, she'd had an exhausting day with two back-to-back closings. The fact it was one of Eric's favorite meals, and he'd helped to make it merely sealed the deal.

Only once, the third night, did she say anything. "I'm going to be big as a house," she said, her lips slowly surrounding a fork filled with homemade ravioli, one of Jake's specialties. She moaned with pleasure and shut her eyes with that dreamy expression he loved.

Fascinated, Jake stared. She was so openly

responsive to food, turning the simple task of eating into an intense sensual experience. He found himself sifting through his collection of old family recipes just to provoke that expression again. He knew this was how Carrie would look when he finally made love to her.

Clearing his throat, he pushed down his own, more prurient, hunger. "I enjoy cooking and don't get a chance to do it often with my schedule. But, if you object, I'll make salads from now on." Hell, she'd probably wilt the lettuce.

She laughed. "When you put it like that, I could never deprive anyone of so much enjoyment."

His husky laughter mingled with hers. He *was* enjoying his vacation, a fact that would shock anyone who knew him. A few weeks ago, he'd have paid six month's salary to avoid time off. Now, there weren't enough hours in the day to spend with Carrie.

She had him lusting one moment, then snuck into his heart the next by simply sitting next to him in front of the television, her fingers buried in Riker's fur. Daniela had dropped the dog off a couple of days earlier and Jake was thrilled to have him back, however, he'd immediately lost the animal to Carrie. Jake was actually jealous of the way the shepherd received all of her hugs and kisses and caresses when she walked in the door, while Jake had to wait in line.

He loved her wit, her smiles and laughter, the way she talked to him. He especially loved the hungry way she looked at him when she didn't think he was watching. He wanted to make her happy, see her grow round with a baby, another great kid like Eric. Or a little cinnamon-haired beauty like her mother.

When he couldn't be with her, he had Eric. With

little effort, the kid had burrowed into Jake's heart, too. They'd developed a tighter relationship than many a father and son could match. They built a dog run off the garage for Riker so he wouldn't have to be confined to the house after Jake went back to work. They installed Jake's new hot tub in one corner of the yard. Between projects they trained Riker, went to the batting cages, hiked the nearby Rocky Mountain trails...and they talked. Several well-placed man-to-man discussions assured Jake that Eric wouldn't head down the same road Mateo had chosen.

He dreaded the end of his vacation. Separating even a small part of himself from Carrie and Eric promised to be difficult. More importantly, he hadn't been able to approach the issue of his job with Carrie. It was his own fault. He'd insisted they place their occupations aside to explore their relationship. But, he'd only delayed the inevitable.

Would he destroy everything when he put on his uniform again? He had five days before he returned to work.

From the kitchen doorway, Jake watched Carrie sip her ice tea. She'd arrived ten minutes ago and now sat on his new living room couch, waiting for the teriyaki chicken he'd thrown on the grill. Her sweet curves were outlined by the rich purple, knit dress she'd worn to work that morning. Her relaxed expression told him how comfortable she'd become with their nightly ritual of winding down together before dinner.

Time to bite the bullet.

He strode into the room and took a seat in the large armchair across from Carrie. "Riker's happily gnawing on a bone. Our dinner will be ready in about twenty minutes."

"I wish you'd let me help make the salad or something." She smiled at him. "I'm getting quite spoiled, you know."

"I love spoiling you. Besides, I'm not the one who worked all day." He looked into her gorgeous caramel eyes and cleared his throat. "While we wait, let's talk about this weekend. Do you have plans for Saturday?"

"It's funny you ask," she said. "Last night, I would have told you I was working. I was supposed to cover a couple of open houses. But today, Sam asked for the time to show a new agent the ropes." She smiled. "I don't have any personal clients scheduled, so I thought I'd take Eric to a movie. Maybe hit our favorite ice cream store for a hot fudge sundae afterward. You want to come with us?"

The knot in his stomach looped tighter. Thankful Sam had jumped on his suggestion to get her out of the office, he was still afraid he was about to cut his own throat by pushing Carrie into a decision she wasn't ready to make. "I have another idea," he said. "I've helped to organize an all-day, services picnic at the park. I'd like to take you and Eric."

She set her ice tea on the heavy, mahogany coffee table between them. "A picnic sounds great, too. But what's a services picnic?"

No turning back now. "It was begun several years ago, so emergency services personnel can get together with their families before the Fourth of July overtime craziness. It includes paramedics, ambulance drivers, firemen and—"

"Policemen," Carrie said flatly. "I see."

Her tight expression propelled him around the

coffee table. He moved her tea aside and sat in front of her, her hands cradled in his palms. "Carrie, I'm a cop. So are most of my friends. Sooner or later, we have to deal with this."

Clouds shadowed her eyes, but he ignored them. If she couldn't tolerate his uniform, she'd never accept the rest. He should have told her about S.W.A.T. long ago. The stakes were higher now that he'd fallen for her. "I return to work on Monday. Do you plan to shut me out again when I put my uniform back on?"

"Of course not."

"Why not?"

"I-I...you're different." Her answer was nearly inaudible, hesitant. "I don't see you that way anymore."

The tension between his shoulder blades eased. "How do you know? You haven't seen my uniform since the day I brought Eric home."

"I see past what you wear." The fact she wouldn't look him in the eye weakened her assurance.

"Then do the same for my friends." He squeezed her fingers. "I can't guarantee there won't be a uniform or two — officers stop in before and after shifts — but I work with good people. Is it fair to automatically categorize all of us?" He knew he'd said the wrong thing when her eyes widened.

She dragged her hands away and scooted down the couch to stand out of his reach. "I don't know any more," she exclaimed. "Why are you pushing this?"

Jake's heart turned into lead in his chest as he, too, stood. "Because you don't know, and you should. Your husband's death was a tragic accident. You have to stop laying blame where it doesn't belong." He'd laid the gauntlet between them. Would she take it up?

"You don't know what you're talking about," she said. "It was no accident that cop shot Tomás in the back."

He shook his head at her analysis of the six-year-old incident, his worst fears realized. He'd wanted her to see the situation clearly, without dredging up everything again, but she'd left him little choice.

Calling on every last ounce of professionalism he could muster, he confronted her with the truth. "I've read the investigative report," he revealed, the file Ramón unearthed for him etched in his mind.

"The truth is there. Hostages were being released. The bank robber had thrown his gun in plain view so S.W.A.T. could secure the situation. There was no indication the man was suicidal."

The color drained from Carrie's face.

Jake's guts twisted. "No one saw the second gun until it was too late. The S.W.A.T. officer had no choice at that point. He had to fire or die.

"In the seconds before he pulled the trigger, the gunman stood alone. According to every witness, it was safe to fire." His voice softened. "Honey, your husband threw himself at the robber. He got in the way. It was a tragic accident."

"No! Tomás wouldn't do that. He promised he'd never leave me. He promised!" Memories ripped through Carrie as if the robbery happened only yesterday, that awful, familiar sense of loss and helplessness swamping her senses. Wiping her hands across her cheeks, she stared in surprise at two wet palms. It had been years since she'd cried.

Jake strode toward her. "Carrie, honey, I'm—"

His way was blocked. A flash of green crossed her

vision. Numb, she watched Eric launch himself at the man who'd become his friend, the closest thing he had to a father.

"You made Mom cry," he yelled, pummeling Jake's broad chest. "You can't hurt her. I won't let you!"

Horrified to see Jake do nothing to protect himself, Carrie ran over and dragged her son away. "Stop it, Eric. This isn't right!"

"He lied, Mom. You said—"

"No," she cried. "Jake didn't lie."

Eric's tirade was halted more effectively by her words than her hands. His gaze met hers. "You lied?"

Until that instant, she hadn't known the vast consequences of her blind stupidity. What had she done to her son? To Jake? She sank to her knees, unable to defend herself.

"Your mom didn't lie, Eric. Not intentionally." Jake hunched beside them. "Haven't you ever wanted to believe something so badly you convinced yourself it was true?"

"I-I guess. Mom?"

The one word smashed through Carrie's shattered composure. Her heart a lead weight, she touched his face with trembling fingers. "I'm sorry, baby," she said. "I never meant to hurt you."

She stood and looked at Jake. "I-I hurt you, t-too." Her voice broke unevenly. "I'm so sorry!" Before she could fall into a thousand pieces at his feet, she ran out the front door.

~~~

Carrie stretched out on a padded lounge chair that had seen better days and took deep breaths of flower-scented night air into her lungs. She sat outside the arc of light generated over the back door and allowed the shadows beneath the eight-foot lilac bush to soften the sharp edges of her mood. Her oriental robe tucked around her, she stared up at the moonlit, midnight sky.

Exhaustion dragged at her senses, but sleep had proven elusive. Only Eric could lay claim to the sleep of the innocent. She was far from innocent, and the blame lay entirely on her shoulders.

It was a miracle her son still spoke to her. Jake must have said something before sending him home with their cooked dinner because Eric spent the evening being so helpful and considerate, she'd wanted to scream at him to stop treating her like a broken doll. It wasn't Eric's fault her view of the world was so skewed.

Digging into the robe's cavernous pocket, she drew out the sheaf of papers that had rested in a shoebox at the back of her closet until several hours ago. She couldn't read in the semi-darkness where she sat but having read the damning thing several times now, the words were burned into her mind. For the first time since receiving the report she'd read it completely, with an open mind.

"Carrie, are you okay?"

Jake. The voice from across the yard should have startled her, but, somehow, she'd known he'd come. She jammed the papers in her robe pocket where the sharp corners dug into her right hip through her satin chemise. "Yes," she said, surreptitiously wiping away her tears. "I'm okay."

Walking across the lawn, he loomed over her. "I saw the light and thought I'd check."

He was a natural protector and probably an excellent policeman as a result. "As you can see, I'm fine."

I don't see physical danger." His gaze swept her from head to toe and back again, settling on her face. "You'll have to convince me the emotional ones aren't there."

The man saw too much. "I can deal with unpalatable truths." Her eyes drifted shut. "Now, anyway."

Jake muttered something that ended with "stubborn woman". Her eyes popped open at the same time he slid onto the lounge beside her. He gathered her to his hard body. How a man so strong could be so tender, she'd never understand. Butterflies took flight in her belly. Her pulse quickened. She wriggled in his embrace, unsure whether she was trying to escape or snuggle deeper.

"Don't struggle," he growled when the lounge squeaked loudly in protest. "This chair doesn't appear too stable. Besides, I need this as much as you do." His breath whispered across her face. He nuzzled her hair and put his large hand over hers where it rested on his chest. "This isn't so hard, is it?"

Jake's wonderful male scent invaded her senses. "No." She felt safe, secure whenever he held her, an illusion not to be trusted, but one she had no energy to resist. She was so tired of running from this man.

Quiet reigned as they gazed at the stars peeking around a few slumberous clouds. It was Jake who broke the silence. "You want to talk about it?"

"Yes. No." A small laugh escaped. "I don't think I'm ready to relinquish my guilt."

"You haven't done anything to feel guilty about."

"I never really accepted what happened," she argued, shaking her head. "It was easier, I guess, to be mad at that policeman than at Tomás. I'll never know why he had to be the hero."

Deep down, though, she did know. Tomás had always been the kind to jump in when someone needed help. He'd picked up the pieces of an insecure eighteen-year-old who'd lost her mother, showered her with the love she desperately needed, gave her a son, and never asked for more than she was willing to give.

Carrie had never truly appreciated the man she'd married until he was gone, which only twisted her guilt tighter. She tilted her head against Jake's shoulder so she could look at his face. "The one I'm truly mad at is me," she confessed. "I've based the last six years of my life on a lie I told myself over and over, until the truth was thoroughly buried."

Jake's fingertips brushed her cheek, then traced along her jaw line. "You're being too hard on yourself."

She frowned as her concentration melted under his touch. "I should. Eric knows next to nothing about his father, his life or death, because I took the easy way. I denied life to all my memories of Tomás. The good, along with the bad. Eric deserves better."

"You'll give him what he needs."

Her inadequacies had become distressingly clear lately. The police report in her robe pocket was a sharp reminder of how badly she'd screwed up. "I wouldn't blame Eric if he never forgave me."

"He loves you. He understands extremely well for a boy his age."

His fingers skimmed the fine hairs at the nape of her neck and sent pleasurable goose bumps skittering down her arms. "I'm glad you're still friends. I never meant to spoil that for you."

"Forget it," he said. "You got everything out in the open. That's what friends are for." His arm squeezed around her waist. "We are still friends, aren't we?"

Her entire body centered on the feel of his lips on her forehead, the heavy thump of his heart beneath her ear. *Say it, Carrie. Tell him it's over. You have nothing more to give, and it's cruel to let him think otherwise.*

Her attempt to pull away was half-hearted at best. Her voice was stronger. "We just can't be friends any more, Jake."

"I agree."

She stilled in his embrace, aware her movements had set the chair swaying beneath them. "You agree?"

In the soft light from the back porch, she watched Jake's lips lift into one of his bone-melting smiles. "We can't be *just* friends any more. I've said all along we're meant to be lovers, too."

The thought of making love with this man was wildly compelling. But could she give in to her desire and still walk away with her heart intact? She couldn't say it was whole now. Jake seemed to be holding bits and pieces of it without her quite knowing how he'd gotten them. "I don't think that's a good idea," she said. "Not after what happened tonight."

He glanced down at the police report sticking out of her robe pocket between them, tugged it free, and tucked it out of sight under the lounge chair. "Okay. Tell me what happened tonight."

What happened? She'd only acknowledged the truth about her husband's death. She'd merely conceded, in her own mind at least, that Joan was right and Jake's uniform was a convenient barrier she'd thrown in front of her attraction to the man. But, more than that, she'd realized every time she thought of her future, she saw Jake in it and she'd sworn to never, ever risk her heart again.

Jake spoke before she could bolster her defenses. "I'll tell you what happened, honey." He gathered her satin robe tie in his hand. "You learned you no longer feel the same way about policemen as you did this morning."

"I, um—" She lost the capacity to breathe as she watched the knot in her belt come undone with one small tug. "That's hardly the point."

His hand dove inside the robe to her hip, bared by the high cut of her panties beneath her chemise. "It's the whole point. The only thing that's keeping you at a distance is your belief in my guilt-by-association." His fingers spread over her bottom and press her body against him. "Now we've eliminated the problem, we take the next step."

A flash fire of longing raced through her thought processes and burned them to ash. "Next step?"

He smoothed his palm up her side, nudging material out of his way until he stopped at the sensitive hollow under her breast. "We spend time together, a lot more time," he said, his voice a husky rasp. "We'll start with the services picnic in the park on Saturday."

His gaze intensified. "Or, if you like," his thumb brushed the curve of her breast, teasing but not quite reaching her aching nipple, "I could always put you under house arrest and make love to you night and day until neither of us can remember our names."

Carrie's pulse snagged on the image he'd created in her mind. Her body and emotions were drawn incredibly taut. As foolish as it seemed, she'd give anything to lose herself in Jake's tender embrace just once. With nothing between them. No uniform. No past. No future. Was it wrong to want one night with Jake to balance against a lifetime of loneliness?

Probably. "I don't know about you," she said, her words a throaty whisper, "but I've got a pretty good memory."

He stilled. The hand that created such wondrous havoc beneath her skin earlier lifted to capture her chin. Her face tilted into the light, he examined her expression. "If I didn't know better," he said, "I'd say you just issued a challenge."

She felt a brief pang of insecurity when hot intent darkened his eyes. "Do you want to make love with me?"

"Desperately," he said, his voice a rumble of need.

Her gaze dropped to his lips. Waves of longing washed over her, reckless, and oh, so deliciously mesmerizing. She'd never known how devastating a man's kiss could be. Until Jake. His lips demanded. They beguiled. They inflamed, until she trembled with desire. She wanted the blaze to consume her. "It's what I want, too, Jake."

"You have to be sure about this, sweetheart. I won't have regrets between us."

No matter what happened after tonight, she needed this time with him as much as she needed her next breath of air. "No regrets."

Smoothing her fingers over the curve of his mouth, her insides fluttered with expectation. "That day after the barbecue," she said, "the last time you kissed me, you said I'd have to beg you for another one." She paused. "I'm begging. Please, Jake? Kiss me?"

His hand tangled in her hair, he eliminated the gap between them. "Do you have any idea how long I've waited to hear you say that?" he rasped just before their lips met.

Carrie didn't even attempt to answer the rhetorical question, too busy reveling in the feel of Jake's mouth moving against hers. Hard and demanding, one moment. Soft and teasing, the next. With each sip, each nip, he dragged her deeper into a pool of desire. Craving more, she threw her arms around his neck.

She'd barely anchored herself when the lounge chair collapsed beneath them. Their mouths jolted apart. Before they hit the ground, Jake yanked her atop him taking the worst of the fall with a grunt. His chest rose and fell beneath her hands, tangled in his shirt where she held on for dear life. His eyelids lowered, he groaned as if in pain.

"Jake!" She wriggled around trying to get off him without injuring him further. "Sweet mercy! Are you okay?"

He groaned again.

It took her a second to realize the sound was layered with laughter. When she looked down into his laughing eyes and confirmed he was all right, she grinned. "Okay, one regret," she quipped. "We should never have started this in a lounge chair on its last legs."

Abruptly setting her aside on one of the tumbled cushions, Jake rolled to his feet and tugged her up into his arms, his laugh rough and masculine. "No regrets," he said into her hair. "Let's take this inside where I can keep you safe."

When the earth moves again, she added in her head.

How they ever made it to the sanctuary of her

bedroom, she didn't know. Every time Jake stopped her for another scorching kiss, she forgot where they were headed and why it was critical they get there. Finally, she was lying on her bed wearing only her chemise and panties, Jake's bare chest pressed against her rapidly thrumming heart.

Jake studied the way the light from the alley drew slim streaks across Carrie's curvaceous form, his restraint nearly spent. Primitive desire urged him to take what he wanted quickly, but this moment was too long in coming. He didn't want to rush now. With one finger, he trailed an exploratory path over one smooth hip to the satin that hid her curves, then up to the lace skimming her heaving breasts.

Was she turned on as much as he was or were second thoughts robbing her of air? "Honey, you can still change your mind," he said. "If you want me to stop, I will." His instincts rejected the outrageous thought, but he'd do it. Somehow.

"Too late." She wove her fingers through his hair. "Much, much too late." Her tongue flicked his earlobe before she nibbled her way down his throat.

Shaken, Jake's body tightened unbearably. He skimmed off her nightgown. Her panties. Then, balanced on the heel of one hand, his gaze grazed her naked body, full breasts and gently curved stomach, down tanned legs to her slim feet and prettily painted, pink toenails. She looked so small beneath him, he was almost afraid to touch her. He swallowed convulsively. "Sweetheart, you're more beautiful than I dreamed."

His cheek brushed the swell of one breast. His lips surrounded the pouting nipple at its peak. Carrie arched into his mouth, and he sucked harder. He moved to the breast on the other side and gave it the same loving caresses.

She moaned. "I need to touch you, too," she said. Her fingers fluttered down from his shoulders to his chest, then his stomach where they fumbled at the top button of his jeans. With her other hand, she rubbed one palm against his erection uncomfortably confined by the thick denim fabric.

With a pained sound, he circled her wrists and tugged them away from his waistband. "No!" He paused to take a calming breath, rested his forehead on hers. "I didn't come over here with protection. Tonight is just for you."

"We can, I mean, you don't have to—"

She stopped when he continued to shake his head and abruptly shoved him over on his back. Draped across him, she opened the drawer next to the bed and took out an unopened box of condoms.

Jake laughed. He couldn't help it. Carrie was a constant surprise. "You keep an extra-large box beside your bed?"

"Joan had a bachelorette party for one of our friends last month. This was my gag gift." Running a fingernail in an erratic circle through the crisp, dark hair on his chest, she shrugged. "I don't think she ever thought I'd use them."

He grinned. He'd never wanted this woman more. She was so damned adorable covered in a blush of embarrassment. "Remind me to kiss Joan next time I see her," he said. His voice thickened when her fingernail traveled into new territory. "In the meantime, this one's yours."

He kept the kiss light for about three seconds. Then,

weeks of pent-up longing took over and the time for talk was gone. Carrie's response was everything he could have imagined. When he slowed his caresses, she whimpered with frustration. Her moans of delight told him when he discovered an erotic zone that commanded more exploration.

Finally ripping open the box of condoms, he grabbed one as she pushed his jeans and underwear down his legs, leaving them tangled in the brass railing at the bottom of the bed. He tossed the box to the bedside table when her fingers clasped around him, barely holding on to the condom he needed as she nibbled her way over his collarbone and downward. She nipped his nipple and he damned near lost it.

Too fast. *Too slow.*

He sucked air into his empty lungs. His heart pounded an impossibly accelerated rhythm as he rode the sensations only Carrie sparked. His blood surged, fierce, out of control. Desperation — a twist of emotions he had no time to identify — demanded he bury himself deep inside her and stake his claim forever.

His hands smoothed over her creamy skin. His hands and mouth explored and tasted until she writhed beneath him.

"No more," she gasped. "Love me, Jake. Now!"

"Soon, honey," he vowed. "We have all night." It sounded good. In principle.

He dipped his tongue into her navel at the same time he thrust a finger inside her moist heat. *So hot. So damned tight.* His need to protect her warred with his desire to possess her.

She jerked, her head thrown back as he stroked two fingers inside her. "Oh!" she whimpered. "Please!" She bucked against his palm, reached for him. Her hand around his aching shaft, she guided him to her. Squeezed her demand.

"Sweetheart, I—"

Muttering an explicit Italian curse, he quickly protected her. "We'll go slower next time," he promised. Then he rocked against her once, twice, before he pressed into her incredible heat, her name a guttural sound in his throat. She felt so tight around him, he eased forward one excruciating inch at a time until he was sheathed to the hilt inside her.

He'd come home.

Carrie's eyes widened at the wondrous feelings crashing over her. Her legs and emotions wound around Jake as she pushed to complete his possession. He was dangerously near the edge. She could sense it. See it in his eyes. It made her feel strong. Powerful. She barely breathed, testing his control with a tentative flex of muscles.

Jake groaned, his back like steel under her fingers. Framing her face in his hands, he began to move. She met the rhythm he created with her own. The pressure inside her built unbearably. When she thought she'd break into a million pieces, she let it happen. Glorious shudders of completion rippled through her again and again as Jake moved faster, until she crested again seconds before he joined her.

They came down together, slowly. A small touch here, a last caress there, a whispered sound of approval, made the descent last. Jake shifted most of his weight on his elbows so she could breathe, but she loved the feel of his muscular body, his skin slick against hers. Loved the way their air mingled as if they were one. The scent of their lovemaking filled her lungs, her body, with satisfaction. If she never came out of this sensual fog, it would be too soon.

Jake recovered first. He kissed the tip of her nose. "You are the most incredible woman." His gaze locked with hers, his voice like gravel. "Do you have any idea what you do to me?"

A trill of alarm skimmed Carrie's spine at the possessive look in his eyes. No! She wasn't ready. Tomorrow was soon enough to deal with the consequences of her weakness. Tonight was hers.

Crushing her anxiety, she shifted beneath Jake and nearly fainted with giddy relief when she felt him respond. She gave him a saucy look. "Oh," she said, kissing the damp skin over his collarbone, "I think I have a pretty good idea. Didn't I hear something about 'next time'?"

He rolled over on the bed so that she straddled his hips. "Mmm." His hands covered her breasts and kneaded them until she felt the tension rise again inside her. "I think the operative word was 'slow'."

Carrie moaned when he pulled her down for a kiss, surrendering once more to the delights of his languid touch.

Chapter Eleven

The weather on Saturday was gorgeous. Carrie flipped aside the curtain on her bedroom window to catch the first streak of crimson to tinge the nearly cloudless sky, on the lookout for rain to cancel today's plans. A strange heaviness hung in the air, as if something dire was about to happen, and she was never more aware of her vulnerability.

Although she'd had three days to get used to the idea of confronting years of irrational behavior, she wished the picnic were behind her. It was easy to analyze one's darkest fears in the shadows of a summer night, but to face them in broad daylight? That was another story. What if she couldn't handle the sight of a cop in uniform, let alone a whole park full of them?

She glanced at her rumpled bed. If only Jake were there now. She'd crawl back under the covers into the safety of his arms. Then, there would be no question of going anywhere, least of all to a picnic she dreaded.

Jake was in his own bed. Now, anyway. He'd reluctantly gone home an hour ago because she wasn't prepared to tell Eric she'd fallen in lo...lust with his batting coach. Somehow, despite her good intentions, one night of exquisite lovemaking had become two, then three. Each night as Eric slept, Carrie sat in the backyard on her new lounge chair waiting for Jake. Each night when they kissed their way up to her bedroom, she promised herself it would be the last. Each night, she broke that vow.

Her desire should have burned out as quickly as it ignited. It only grew stronger and brighter every time Jake loved her, smoldering when they were apart, blazing out of control when they were together. She knew she was taking too many chances with her heart, but pushed away the niggling worry whenever it reared its ugly head.

The truth was, once she crossed the line there was no going back. Alone too long, she desperately needed these fleeting hours with Jake. He gave her so much comfort and strength and understanding. He listened to her concerns about Eric, about work, even encouraged her to share her memories of her childhood. Of Tomás. Then, Jake made such sweet love to her, she didn't know where she left off and he began. Only for Jake would she risk confronting her painful memories head-on and step inside his world for a few hours.

By nine o'clock, she was at the park helping him to transfer a mass of game equipment and casserole dishes from the car to the reserved picnic area where four industrial-sized grills and two smokers were already set up near the huge open-sided pavilion that shaded more than twenty picnic tables. She'd hardly caught her breath when Eric disappeared into the trees with several other boys in a blur of jeans and sneakers.

"He'll be fine, honey," Jake said, his arm loose around her waist. "He knows the rules."

She smiled at how easily her son had taken Jake's orders. "Maybe you should write them down. You gave him so many rules before he left, I'm not sure what's allowed."

He kissed the tip of her nose. "Tell you what, I'll keep track of his boundaries. You keep track of yours."

Her eyebrows rose. "I have boundaries?"

Jake chuckled. "Not with me," he said, walking away.

"I ran into that one, didn't I?" she said under her breath. Her lips twitched as she followed the man with the sinful brown eyes.

They joined the small crowd milling around the grills. Jake introduced everyone within range, but she asked him to stop when her brain began to twist up the names. She eventually settled down with his partner, Ramón Herrera, and his wife, Maria, at a prep table slicing cheese a local dairy had donated.

She watched Jake set up children's games several yards away. The man might put his pants on the same way as every other man, as Joan suggested, but his stonewashed jeans molded his hips and legs in a way that made her pulse hitch. And, very few men could pull off wearing the colorful red-white-and-blue cotton shirt he'd tucked into his waistband. Masculinity and confidence oozed from every pore in Jake's body, and her fingers itched to go exploring.

"Better let me have that slicer before you cut off something important," Maria quipped from across the picnic table.

Her fantasy disrupted, Carrie carefully set the slicer aside and eyed the mountain of cheese in front of her. "I'm done anyway."

"I'd say Jake's the one who's done."

"Excuse me?"

"I'm sorry. I thought, you two are an item, aren't you?" She frowned. "It's obvious that—"

"Tactful, Maria," Ramón commented. He shook his head and left the prep table with a platter of cheese balanced on each hand.

Maria stuck her tongue out at her retreating husband's back and called out. "You were wondering, too. Don't say you weren't." She grinned at Carrie. "Men! Anyone with half a brain can see how much you love that man over there." She nodded in Jake's direction. "You don't know how happy that makes me. I've been so worried about him."

Love? Carrie picked at the concept in her mind. Unable to force the notion back into its proper mental cubbyhole—the one reserved for impossible dreams—she focused on the other woman's expression. "You really are worried about Jake. Why?"

"That man, the hours he works! He lived with us for four months before he bought his house and I barely saw him." She rolled her eyes dramatically. "I think he takes on all the extra shifts because he doesn't have anything better to do. It isn't good to work so much. Jake needs someone to make him want to come home at night."

"Maria, *mi corazón*." Ramón came up behind his wife and folded his arms around her. He kissed her temple, a warning in his voice. "Jake took his vacation. Let it go."

"It only took two years and an official decree, *mi amor*." She leaned back into her husband's embrace and smiled at Carrie. "I'm not saying anything that isn't common knowledge. Down at the station, everyone was so sure Jake couldn't stick it out and stay away, they had a pool on how long he'd last."

Carrie knew all about the man's persistence. He'd gotten past her defenses, something she'd thought impregnable. "Who won the bet?"

"We decided to donate the pool to the picnic fund," Ramón said. "Except for a few organizational calls for today, Jake hasn't gone near the station. A few of the guys were beginning to wonder if he'd fallen off the face of the earth."

"I'd say he had a good reason to disappear." Maria patted her husband's arms to release her and reached for a package on the table. She waved a knife in Carrie's direction, then turned it on the tomatoes. "Jake's a good man, a family man," she said, not looking up from her task. "I'm sure he won't work so much, now that he has you."

If he doesn't have you, what then?

The question lingered too long in Carrie's mind. It was not her place to worry about Jake's work habits. Worry worked alongside love and...darn it, there was that word again! She shied away from it. Someone else, some other woman would have to keep Jake from pushing himself beyond good sense and safety.

She watched him place an orange cone on an obstacle course for the older children, trying to imagine what this other woman might look like. The picture couldn't form because Jake glanced up, flashed his captivating, come-and-get-me smile, and her heart pounded the thought out of her head. It was a nice dream—Jake, coming home to her and Eric every night—but a dream nonetheless.

Carrie sighed and forced her thoughts elsewhere. She watched several boys kick a soccer ball around. She smiled at a teenage girl playing with a puppy in the grass. Her gaze skimmed the nearby groups until it was caught by the appearance of a very pregnant woman being helped by her husband into a lawn chair. Two small children jumped up and down impatiently while their mother was seated.

Unable to decide what bothered her about this particular scene, she stared. The woman was unfamiliar. The boy and girl weren't old enough to attend Eric's school, although the boy might be in kindergarten. Pursing her lips, Carrie studied the children's father.

There was nothing distinctive about him either. He was in his thirties from what she could tell around the mirrored sunglasses that hid his eyes. A baseball cap covered most of his buzz-cut, blond hair. She could only see his smiling profile, but her sense of familiarity grew. "Who's that over there?"

Maria shaded her eyes with one hand and followed Carrie's nod in the man's direction. "That's Stan Murcheson. He's a detective. You know him?"

No, she didn't. But she'd seen his picture, read his name, in the six-year-old investigative report now tucked neatly back in a shoebox in her closet. She was staring at the S.W.A.T. officer responsible for her husband's death.

Freezing from the inside out, Carrie braced against the onslaught of pain she knew would come.

~~~

Something's wrong.

Jake stopped several feet away from the picnic table where he'd left Carrie with his friends, a large bag of game equipment clamped in one hand. She was looking at something beyond him. Her expression reminded him of a Siamese kitten he'd once rescued from an over-exuberant Great Dane. Confusion and alarm mixed with a huge dose of shock.

Squinting against the sun's glare, he followed her gaze directly to the one person he hadn't expected to see. He strangled on one of his more vitriolic curses. Murcheson was supposed to be fishing in Oregon! Why was he here?

One look at Stan's extremely pregnant wife and Jake had his answer. Damn it all to hell!

It didn't matter how such a stupid twist in circumstances happened. It was the woman in front of him that he had to get out of harm's way. Ramón, aware of Carrie's history because of the report he'd pulled for Jake, raised an eyebrow at him and nodded once, their private signal questioning if he needed backup.

Jake shook his head and tightened his grip on the canvas bag. He approached the picnic table. "Hey, Carrie, how about giving me a hand with these bats?" He held them up for inspection. "My arm's about to fall off."

She stared at him blankly before she rose and grabbed one of the bag handles. "Sure."

Walking in the opposite direction from the ball field, Jake led her to a stand of cottonwoods out of sight of the others before he stopped. "Are you all right, honey? Do you want me to take you home?"

"No. I mean, I'm fine. I want to stay." Then, she blurted, "He's the one, isn't he?"

Jake nodded. The need to touch her prompted him to remove her hand from the bat bag so he could drop it at their feet. Cradling the back of her neck, he tugged her flush against him. He stroked his thumb along the delicate skin beneath her ear. "I'm sorry, honey. Murcheson wasn't supposed to be here today. I'd never have brought you otherwise."

She nuzzled his wrist, soothing and stirring him at the same time. "It doesn't matter."

"Of course, it matters." Jake was angry with himself. He should have double-checked his sources.

"That's just it. I don't think it does." Carrie's slim hand stroked his chest in an oddly reassuring circle. "When I first realized who he was, I wanted to hide so I wouldn't have to face the pain.

"But, it didn't come." A bright smile cleared her expression as she suddenly, exuberantly, threw her arms around his neck and hugged him. "It didn't come, Jake!"

As if a pressure valve within her had been somehow released, her words ran together. "I can't say I felt nothing...that would be expecting too much...but I looked at that man and all I saw was a normal, solicitous husband and father...not the vicious monster I'd created in my mind." She stopped and kissed him.

Jake kissed her back, a reward and a celebration. He wanted to pull her to the ground and make love to her in the sunlight, banish the last of the shadows between them.

Carrie must have had the same idea. She pressed her yielding curves into his hardness. Her hands wove through his hair. Her spiced floral fragrance filled his lungs, insistent and earthy. Her thigh tucked between his legs, she rubbed against him.

He groaned and coaxed her lips apart. He plunged his tongue inside her mouth, mimicking the way he wanted to thrust inside her like he hadn't just left her bed a few hours ago. He could lose himself in this woman. A shout of laughter reminded him there were two hundred people nearby, many of whom were law enforcement co-workers. He chuckled, fully aroused and frustrated beyond belief. "I haven't tried to make love in the bushes since I was seventeen."

"Tried?" Her caramel eyes soft, she wiggled her eyebrows up and down suggestively. "Do you want to succeed this time?"

"I'd like nothing more, sweetheart," he said with a rough laugh. "But we'd better behave. My superiors might find it hard to believe I'm fit to return to work on Monday if I'm cited for lewd behavior in a public place."

The reminder their time together was almost over made Carrie's heart flutter. The last thing she wanted to do was separate herself from Jake's solid, reassuring length, but she forced herself to stand on her own two feet. "I'm glad you brought me today."

"I am, too." His hand covered hers before she could slip away, captured her against him. "I'm proud of you, honey. I know how difficult it's been for you to deal with what happened to Tomás. I'd begun to wonder if my uniform would always be a barrier between us."

Aware the dire, unsettled feeling she'd experienced before dawn this morning had just taken a troubling form, Carrie looked away. A serious discussion of their relationship wasn't a good idea. Her vulnerability had been tested enough for one day. "I don't know why you put up with me," she quipped, stepping back.

Jake leaned over and picked up the bag he'd dropped at their feet. "If I didn't have to get these bats to the ball field," he growled, "I'd finish what we started and show you why."

Carrie knew what he wanted to hear, but the words dried up in her mouth, unformed. She swallowed. "I think I'll stay here a few minutes longer."

"Here. In the bushes."

"I couldn't be safer," she replied. "One shout and Riverton's finest will be at my feet."

"Sweetheart, at least one of them will be." Jake yanked her back into his arms for another searing kiss that branded her, body and soul. When he lifted his head, he tapped a playful fingertip against her nose. "Tell the rest of them to go away and find their own woman."

Smiling foolishly, Carrie watched him walk away, his long stride bold, purposeful. She considered calling him back, but when he passed the group that included Murcheson and his growing family, said something to the detective that made him laugh, her troubled thoughts returned with a vengeance.

Her smile faded as she watched the detective toss a multi-colored beach ball to his two-year-old daughter, then wrestle with his son on the grass in a mock tackle. His wife's laughter rippled across the park to Carrie's ears. Her eyes stung at the sweet impact of their love for each other, and she wondered what might have happened to the man's family if he hadn't pulled the trigger in the bank that day.

Sitting on a bench at the base of a cottonwood, she tried to push the question away. It wouldn't be budged. The answer was playing in the sunlight directly in front of her, and it didn't leave her feeling the least bit comfortable. In fact, the bells in her head finally rang a peal of doom.

The truth is a different set of circumstances didn't

guarantee Tomás would be at her side today. Detective Murcheson, however, wouldn't be here. The report was clear on that point. If he hadn't fired in self-defense six years ago the pregnant woman across the grass would be a widow, not weeks away from childbirth. The two children playing with their daddy would never have been born.

Scanning the happy families scattered through the park, Carrie cringed. How did they cope with the uncertainty that came with living with a cop, the risk of losing their loved ones in the blink of an eye? She knew the pain of growing up with only pictures to love her back. She'd lost her parents. Tomás. Her son was growing up without his father. Had she really thought coming here today changed anything?

She'd come full circle. She'd ignored the way her heart was subconsciously looking for ways to connect her life to Jake's. Until now, the dream hadn't seemed so unreal. She couldn't say Jake's uniform didn't make a difference anymore. It did.

Maybe not in the way she'd thought, but who knew she'd get this deeply involved with the man? How could a uniform be so intricately tied to both her past and her future? How could she risk loving Jake if she wasn't willing to risk losing him?

You already love him.

No! What she felt was desire. Nothing more. She'd stepped into dangerous territory without knowing all the rules. Falling in love was out of the question.

Then, stop being selfish. Jake deserves a whole woman. He deserves love and a family to come home to every night. Walk away before you convince yourself you can give him what he needs.

Her breath caught on the painful edge of reality. How she'd do it, she hadn't a clue, but tonight her relationship with Jake had to end. He'd return to his world on Monday. She had to let him go back to that world. Alone.

Staring at the spot where Jake had stood ten minutes ago, she could already feel the emptiness in her arms, the fading memory of his lips on hers. Sweet mercy, this was going to hurt like hell.

~~~

"Jake, let go!" Carrie struggled in his arms, exasperated beyond good manners. Four hours in an overflowing emergency room after a disastrous baseball game was bad enough, but if Jake insisted on carrying her everywhere she was going to lose her mind.

Jake's jaw clenched ominously. He took another resolute step toward his destination, his own front door.

Carrie worked to calm herself. Glancing around, she was relieved to see their neighbors had retired to their beds or televisions for the evening. With the ridiculous predicament she'd gotten herself into, who needed witnesses?

"I can walk, Jake. The nurse gave me crutches, and my ankle doesn't hurt any more. In fact, it's kind of numb."

He stopped to look down at her. "That just means the bandage is wound too tight. I told that nurse —"

Carrie placed her fingers over his mouth. "It's not wound too tight. The man knew what he was doing."

Jake snorted. "I'll check for myself when we get inside." He scowled. "You can stop arguing with me about this. You and I both heard what the doctor said."

"I can't believe you lied about being my husband."

176

Her heart skipped at the memory despite strict orders from the sane part of her that reminded her she was supposed to walk away from the man.

"How else was I going to hear what he had to say? You would have hopped right out the door, no matter what he said, if I hadn't been there."

"I'm surprised you didn't flash your badge at him," she grumbled.

"I would have if he hadn't relented." He took a deep breath. "Honey, your ankle is sprained. I'll lay odds the rest of your body is protesting rather loudly right now, too, so take your damned independence and put it away for a while. I'm carrying you into the house."

Carrie was hard-pressed to find a portion of her body that didn't hurt. But telling Jake that would only make him more intractable than he'd been since she injured herself.

She studied him through her lashes. This was a side of Jake she'd seldom seen, the side she suspected was reserved for the demands of police work. He was coolly commanding, a bristling bear growling his dominance. The urge to cuddle up to him and smooth his ruffled fur was overwhelming. "I'm sorry, Jake."

He stopped at the bottom of his front steps to look down at her. "I'm being a jerk, aren't I? When I saw you laid out on the ground like that—"

His expression hardened. "I'll never forgive myself for running into you. I damn near killed you."

The man's protective urges had kicked in with a vengeance. He blamed himself for her injuries, although it truly wasn't his fault. She hadn't played ball since high school. But she didn't want to think about how she was going to break things off with her captivating neighbor when the day was over either, so she'd joined a team to keep her hands and mind busy. That was her first mistake.

She made her second mistake when she ran in from left field to cover the shortstop, tripped over her own two feet, and stumbled in front of Jake racing for third base. The poor man tried to stop, but it was too late. He'd run over her like a steam roller. By the time her ears stopped ringing and she'd caught her breath, he was hovering over her like an avenging angel.

"Even if you were able to stop, you couldn't have protected me from my own klutziness." She stroked her hand against his tight jaw. "I'm okay."

"I'm making sure of it." He adjusted his grip under her knees and glanced at her son. "Eric, if you'll open the door, we'll get your mom settled."

The boy rushed to do his bidding.

Carrie ached from head to toe, no one would listen to her, and Eric had abandoned her to take Jake's side. Only irritation stood between her and a serious crying jag. "I'm not staying here," she declared, her chin stuck out.

"Please, Mom. Just tonight? I don't know what to do."

In the face of her son's anxious expression, her defiance collapsed. The poor kid had never seen his mom hurt before. "Okay, Eric. We'll stay," she said, peeking up at Jake.

His gaze held hers. "Can we go in now?"

Self-conscious, she shrugged. "Your arms are probably getting tired."

He lifted her higher to whisper into her ear. "I don't suppose it's occurred to you I might never tire of having you in my arms."

For the life of her, she couldn't answer. Her own sense of self-preservation demanded she remain silent.

Within minutes she was resting on Jake's comfortable sofa, a pillow behind her back, another one under her sprained ankle, Riker's big puppy dog eyes fixed on her every move. Eric dashed across the street to their house with a list of necessities in his hand. Jake disappeared into the kitchen to serve the Chinese takeout he'd picked up on their way home since they'd missed out on dinner.

Carrie didn't have any choice but to submit to the willful male fussing. If she didn't have the strength to crawl away, she decided in a fit of pique, she definitely wasn't strong enough to break off with Jake tonight. "Coward," she whispered to the empty room.

Riker whined and laid his heavy head in her lap so she couldn't move. She smiled down at the shepherd. "It's okay, boy," she scratched behind his ears, "I'm not going anywhere." *Not yet.*

~~~

She was trapped in a deep, black cave, hemmed in by thousands of tiny green imps with five-hundred-pound hammers and nasty smiles. So far, she'd managed to control the pressure of their tightening circle, but periodically, one would sidle in and give her body a resounding whack, reminding her of her growing weariness. Sooner or later, the little demons would run rampant, unchecked, but...

It was the biggest one, winding steel gossamer around her ankles, which worried her the most. She'd never escape the pain if her feet were tied. She cried out for him to stop.

"Shh, honey. It's okay," he replied, throwing another loop.

Frowning, she realized her demon had delicious chocolate eyes, a sinful grin, and a voice to melt her heart. Her eyes opened. "Jake?"

"Right here, honey." Finishing his adjustment of the blanket over her legs, he shifted so she could see him without straining.

When he crouched beside her, she relaxed. "You wouldn't believe the dream I was having." Her head shook before she registered the waking pain. "Oh!"

Jake brushed her hair off her forehead. "Ready for that pill now?"

That took some real thought. "No, thanks. I hate pills." She blinked. "I could use some help sitting up though. Nothing seems to be working."

He eased his hands under her, which caused her to gasp. "I feel like I've been run over by a Mack truck."

"No Mack truck." He plumped a pillow behind her. "Just me."

"No Mack truck, just you," she repeated. Then, considering the aptness of the image and the effect this man seemed to have on her emotions, she giggled.

Rocking back on his heels, Jake scowled. "Hey! Are you all right?"

"Mack truck. Jake Stefani. Don't you get it?" She laughed a second time, but paid for it. A sharp twinge in her ribs made her wince.

"No," he said shortly, his gaze critical. "I knew the doctor was too young to know what he was doing." He held up his hand. "How many fingers do you see?"

"Three. Now, stop checking. I'm banged up, not brain damaged." She flexed her shoulders with great

180

care. "What I wouldn't give for a spa and a gentle masseuse."

Jake snapped his fingers. "That I can do! Don't go anywhere." He stood abruptly and ran up the stairs.

When he came back, her oriental robe dangled from his fingertips. "Eric couldn't find your swimsuit. But, if you want to slip into this, you can be the first to try out my new hot tub."

"It's ready?" Eric had told her he and Jake had connected the last bit of pipe a few days ago, but she hadn't known the tub was filled and heated.

Jake nodded. "When I checked the gauge before we left for the park, it was steady at one hundred and two degrees."

It was all too easy to visualize the two of them in the tub. Together. Naked. The water cooling around them as they simultaneously reached for the searing flame which always burned at the heart of their lovemaking.

She clutched at normalcy. "Where's Eric and Riker?" When she'd dozed off, her son was lying on the floor at her feet watching television alongside the German shepherd.

"I chased them upstairs around ten o'clock. Eric was going to hover over you all night, but he was exhausted. He went down for the count after I swore to take care of you. Last time I checked, he and Riker were curled around each other."

"Oh, no! I'm sorry. Eric should know better than to take the dog to bed with him."

Jake shrugged. "I think that became a moot point the first time Riker jumped into the bed after I set it up in the spare room. As long as he stays out of our bed," his gaze locked on her face, "I can live with it."

Our bed. Sweet mercy! Carrie didn't know how to respond to the imagery he'd just laid between them.

Jake waved her robe at her like he hadn't just thrown her intentions into complete disarray. "So, how does that soak sound?"

She surrendered, shivering with anticipation of all that heat. "Like my idea of paradise," she said huskily, not thinking of hot water.

While he went back upstairs muttering something about towels, she struggled to remove her clothes and the bandage wound around her ankle. Just as she finished knotting her hair on top of her head, Jake came back and carried her out the back door to the corner that housed the tub. Removing the lid, he efficiently peeled the robe off Carrie and lowered her into the steaming water.

Chapter Twelve

A camp lantern hung from a long spike on the fence. Jake lit it with a match from his pocket. The flame flickered and sputtered, then settled into a steady glow. "Be right back," he said, returning to the house again.

Carrie sank down until her head rested on the smooth edge and the water lapped the bottom of her chin. She moaned. Bliss! This was better than a pill any day.

She drifted dreamily in the water, her entire body melting. A fine sheen of sweat formed on her forehead, but cooled quickly in the night air. She wiggled her uninjured right foot, the water flowing between her toes. Such a decadent feeling. Nothing felt this good.

Staring at the star-studded sky through the steam eddying lazily around her, her mind provided all sorts of things which felt as good. Jake's kisses melted her bones, too. His touch scorched her skin, while his protective nature soothed her soul. One intriguing smile, one demanding kiss in the park, and she was ready to drag him into the bushes.

He had her twisted in so many knots she was in danger of unraveling. It got worse each time she was with the man. He'd healed innumerable wounds on her battered heart and dismantled her defenses, one by one.

He'd forced her to face her worst fears and change her view of the world. He had her thinking about futures. Of someone to hold onto and grow old with, of love, wedding bells and babies.

Her head slid off the edge of the tub at the thought of church weddings and babies with Jake's laughing eyes. She came out of the water, gasping and choking.

"Better watch yourself, or you'll drown," Jake said from above her.

Too late.

Carrie managed to open one eye in time to see Jake ease his body into the tub across from her. Between the strands of hair that clung wetly to her face, she got a tantalizing view of hairy legs and cutoffs before they were covered by steamy water. She pushed her hair back with unsteady fingers. "Hi," she croaked.

"Hi, yourself." He smiled. "How do you feel?"

Her body was numb, her brain muddled.

Jake flicked a finger at the water, spraying her with droplets. "Is the water helping at all?"

Carrie bit her tongue hard enough to get it moving. "If this doesn't untie my muscles, nothing will."

"A massage ought to just about finish things off then." He whirled his index finger in the air. "Turn around."

Reading the steadiness of his gaze, she did as he instructed. The mere thought of her nakedness, of Jake's imminent touch, had her flushed and bothered in seconds. That he appeared unaffected was unfair and more than a little irritating. Even worse, he'd put on shorts as though he felt it necessary to make his disinterest crystal clear. She didn't know whether to be hurt or miffed.

184

Her thoughts scattered when he guided her arms up to rest on the tub lip. Beginning on one side, he gently massaged her hand, then up her arm to her shoulder. Shifting to the other side, he did the same thing before his fingers worked the cramped muscles between her shoulders.

Aches dissipated under his ministrations, left contentment in its wake. "I was only kidding about the masseuse," she mumbled. "I've never had a genuine massage before." She could get used to this!

"I've never given one," Jake said, his words a deep rumble in her ear. "That makes us even." The ball of his hand pushed up the length of her spine again and again. He pressed harder with each stroke. "Tell me if I hurt you."

She nodded. She knew Jake would never hurt her. Not intentionally. Just as she could never intentionally hurt him. In the deep recesses of her mind, she knew what that meant, but she refused to analyze anything complicated tonight. Nothing would change the fact her heart had taken firm control over her brain, and it was waving a huge, white flag of surrender.

~~~

Jake dragged his hands from Carrie's slippery skin, threw his head back to take a cleansing breath of air, and mentally patted himself on the back for his self-restraint. When he'd offered his tub, he'd ordered his libido into the deep freeze. Carrie would get this massage if it killed him.

A real possibility, Stefani. Have you noticed the unsteadiness in your hands? How about what's going on below the waterline?

He adjusted his cutoffs. Okay, so this was more

185

torture than he'd envisioned. Touching Carrie without *really* touching her was a test of inhuman proportions. However, he couldn't just quit because the denim he'd put between them was confining. He had to blank his mind, get it done, then tuck her into his bed. Alone.

"Jake?" Carrie glanced over her shoulder.

Flexing his fingers, he got off his knees and sat on the bench. "Move this way," he said with a tight smile, "and hand over a leg."

Her undamaged ankle cradled in one hand, he managed a credible massage from the tip of her pretty, pink-tinted toes right up to her hip. Letting the leg drift, Jake attributed the dizzying rush of blood in his veins to the heat of the water. He was a goner if he acknowledged anything else.

He could do this. No problem. Only one leg left.

He was a goner, for sure.

The sight of Carrie's bruised, swollen ankle should have doused the fire in his groin, but his gaze fixed on the mole that had taunted him for weeks now. That wickedly flashing mole. Demanding attention. Petitioning his surrender.

Start here!

The summons beat against his beleaguered control. Of all the ways he'd made love to Carrie, he'd never started there. Somehow, postponing the impulse had only amplified the desire.

Jake blinked. He couldn't do justice to that particular fantasy, not under these circumstances. Resigned, he lifted the ankle above the waterline and pressed his mouth to the mole in a silent vow to return.

His kiss was so light Carrie didn't open her eyes. Her cheek remained propped against the side of the tub, allowing him to stare at her long lashes, spiky against her flushed skin, the damp tendrils of her upswept hair that curled around her temples. His breath caught when he saw moist steam where he longed to be, clinging to her lush lips.

They parted in unconscious invitation, and he stopped breathing altogether. Had she fallen asleep? "Carrie?"

When her eyes opened, he saw his own hunger reflected there. There was no stopping what he did next even if it meant saving his life. With a palm under her knee, he guided her into his lap. Just one kiss, he told himself. A real one to get him through the night.

It was his last coherent thought. Carrie said his name in that breathless way that drove him nuts and his fate was sealed. The kiss went on and on, each caress building on the next. His tongue dipped into her mouth to capture her sweetness. To taste her desire for him. Rocked to the core when he found it, he lifted his head to suck air into his empty lungs.

She moaned. "Don't stop."

"Sweetheart, that's the last thing I intend to do."

Slipping off the bench to his knees in the center of the tub where her ankle wouldn't be jarred, he turned her to straddle his waist. Her breasts bumped into his naked chest, retreated, then returned on the next ripple of hot water. He grazed his left hand down her back over her hip to steady her. "I could spend the entire night like this," he said, "just holding you. Touching you. Listening to your sounds of pleasure." With trembling fingers, he caught the nipple that peeked above the water at him and rolled it into a hard knot.

With a gasp, Carrie arched deeper into his hand. The

storm on her senses tugged at the endless ache inside her that had little to do with her injuries. She was no longer amazed at Jake's ability to reduce her to a steamy puddle at his feet with a simple flick of a finger. How she'd ever resisted her feelings in the first place, now that was amazing.

She shared the delicious torment, spreading tiny, biting kisses the length of Jake's jaw. Her hands trailed over his muscular form, shaping, stroking, her mouth following an alternate path. She kissed him to the waterline. Both hands dove beneath it.

Circling her wrists, he lifted her hands out of the water away from his clenched stomach. "Wait," he croaked, his voice raw.

Carrie felt the quake of his fingers on her pulse, the heave of his chest against her breasts, the draw of her power over him. It was always like this with Jake. Exhilarating. Devouring. Breathless. She opened her mouth over his to give him the last of her air. Her tongue brushed, parried. Challenged his control.

His groan vibrated through her body. "Honey, we've got to slow down or you'll get hurt."

Frightened as she was of that eventuality—the feelings and dreams this man had reawakened in her heart made it a certainty—she couldn't tear herself away. "I want you, Jake." She strained forward to lick a trickle of water from his collarbone.

His chin lifted to allow her freer access to his throat. "But your ankle, ahhh, your back—"

"I'll let you know when something hurts," she promised, rocking against the front of his cutoffs. Her voice lowered, throaty, deep. "Mmm, Jake, why aren't you naked?"

"I—" His five o'clock shadow scraped over her shoulder, a mini-line of fire. "I needed help to—"

Her hands escaped his light hold and quietly dipped back into the water. When Jake did nothing to stop her this time, she popped the top button at his waist. "Help to what?" She eased the zipper down.

"To —"

He groaned when the zipper stopped moving and she took him in her hand. His eyes narrowed, glittering and dangerous in the lamplight. "To hell with it," he growled, searing her mouth with a fiery kiss.

An eternity later, Jake's cutoffs sailed over his shoulder into the grass. His hands cupped her bare bottom. Slowly, too slowly, he drew her to him.

Nothing between them, but hot water and even hotter desire, Carrie moved against his erection, her moan lost in the rough sound that rumbled from his throat. A mixture of scents—chlorine and fresh-cut grass, bougainvillea and aroused male—registered in her brain before her breathing became too shallow to sustain the effort.

"You're so sweet, Carrie," Jake said thickly. His thumb measured a bruise marring her upper arm. "I'm afraid to touch you."

"I won't break."

His tongue tenderly rasped the pulse in her neck, then dipped lower. Suddenly, she wasn't sure she spoke the truth. She could break into a million pieces and die happily in his embrace. "Oh, please!"

Lifting her, his hot mouth fastened possessively over one pert nipple. He sucked on the tip for long, exquisite moments, the sensation tugging deep into her belly between her thighs. He cupped her, caressed her, slowly at first, then faster. Teasing her to the edge again and again he stopped her short of her goal each time.

Her nerve endings hummed. The ache intensified unbearably. "Jake, I'm—" Unable to put more than two words together, she raked her fingernails through his chest hair and whimpered her impatience to wrap herself around him.

"Not this time." He held her motionless and kissed her. His mouth teased, coaxed, promised wicked delights, then slipped away leaving her craving more. "You wouldn't believe the fantasies you're fulfilling," he whispered, his gaze locked on her face.

The words were lost when two fingers slid into her heat and toppled her over the precipice. With a guttural cry, she mindlessly rode the unrelenting waves, peaking ever higher until she thought she might drown in ecstasy. "Jake, I...oh...don't leave me!"

"Don't worry, honey." He kissed her. "I'm not going anywhere." He stroked her until the shudders slowed.

She rested her forehead on his damp shoulder, content. Sated. Her whole body boneless. Her lashes felt extraordinarily heavy when she lifted them at last. "I'm sorry. You didn't—"

His chuckle sounded rusty. "I'm not sorry," he said, smoothing her damp hair off her face. "I love to watch you fly apart when I touch you."

Aware of the hard ridge beneath her, she felt the fever rise once again. Only this time, she intended to take this wonderful, irresistible man with her. Her actions were deliberate and far from subtle.

"Ah, sweetheart," Jake grumbled, "it's not fair to take advantage of a man in my weakened condition."

Carrie nipped at his bottom lip. "Take me to your

bedroom and I'll show you fair." Her voice softened to a whisper. "I have to warn you though, it could take a while. Maybe all night."

He shut his eyes against her challenge, silent so long she was afraid she'd gone too far, revealed too much of her hunger, her unbearable need for both physical and emotional intimacy. She read the struggle that raged in his head in the expressions sweeping, one after another, across his face. Indecision was the easiest to identify.

Framing her face in his large hands, he leveled her with a look that delved into her very soul and possessed her. Then he kissed her until her toes curled. "Sweetheart," he growled when he let her come up for air, "you will be the death of me."

Abruptly standing, he lifted her from the tub. Without another word, he strode toward the back door, her arms around his neck, both of them dripping wet and stark naked. He blew out the lamp as he passed so she didn't remind him he'd left behind a pair of cutoffs, a robe, two perfectly dry towels, and one uncovered hot tub.

Some things were simply more important.

~~~

Without turning over or opening her eyes, Carrie intuitively knew two things. She had overslept, and she was alone in the bed. The heat of the sun on the back of her neck informed her of the first. As for the second, there hadn't been a day in weeks when she wasn't acutely aware of Jake's presence, or his absence.

She knew the day must be faced eventually, but she felt too marvelously languorous to greet the world just yet. Besides, she could tell this was one of those mornings when her body needed a slow, gentle warm up. She ached everywhere. One muscle at a time, she stretched the worst of the kinks from her limbs.

The Egyptian cotton sheet wrapped around her body like a warm, lazy lover. Her lips curved. Not that lazy would ever be her lover's style. Jake was energetic, creative, even incurably romantic. But, lazy? Not a chance.

After last night, she'd never again think of moles and freckles in quite the same way. When he'd carried her upstairs, she'd been surprised to see he'd re-decorated his bedroom since his illness. An almost feminine oasis of cream-colored walls, rich cinnamon and nutmeg fabric shades, candles, and flowers had softened the sparse utilitarian look. Mama's influence, or someone else? Like he knew where her thoughts were headed, he smiled crookedly. "I hope you like the colors," he said. "When I picked them out, I imagined you here."

Using a rosebud from the vase on the bedside dresser, Jake had then played a sensuous game of connect-the-dot on her skin, from head to toe and back again, trailing the most sinful sensations in his wake. Sure, she'd reached the pinnacle of delight, she discovered it doubled after she confiscated the flower and drew equally intricate pictures over Jake's body.

Her face buried in the pillow. Lingering traces of their lovemaking teased her nose, triggered nerve endings to eager readiness. Her nipples hardened. She sighed, still unused to this sensual creature she'd become in recent weeks. She'd awakened one day to find this new woman under her skin, one preoccupied with needs and wants, by passion and desire, and it was all fueled by Jake.

Despite what she wanted to believe, it wasn't merely lust either. Jake had reached directly into her empty heart. He'd filled it with his thoughtfulness, his strength and support and, somewhere along the line, it had overflowed and she'd fallen for the man. She was dangerously happy, in love with a cop, and so darned scared. What was she going to do?

"Rise and shine, Mom."

"Go 'way," she mumbled, addressing both her son and the chaotic notions scrabbling around in her brain. She jammed the pillow over her head.

Neither the thoughts nor her son would be muffled. "Mom, get up. It's noon. We've been waiting forever."

Carrie's eyelids cracked open as Eric lifted a pillow corner to peer at her face. "Eric, I don't...wait. What time did you say it was?"

"Twelve," he said. "If you hurry up and eat breakfast, we can watch Godzilla vs. The Sea Monster on the one o'clock movie."

The dose of reality was too much. Carrie rolled onto her back and threw the pillow off the bed. "Sam's going to kill me."

"No, he's not," Jake commented from the open doorway.

Too busy tucking the sheet around her nakedness, Carrie hadn't seen him enter the room. She watched him approach, a tray balanced on his hands. Her skin grew hot and shivery when she saw the single red rose nestled in the center of an irregularly folded, paper napkin.

Was it the same rose Jake had...that she'd...?

Her brain spontaneously brushed away the sight of his short-sleeved cotton shirt tucked into his favorite worn blue jeans. The naughty thing followed that vision

193

with the memory of dragging the fragrant bloom over his tanned skin, watching the soft petals snag and caress his muscular body. A different kind of ache tugged at her lower belly.

Her pulse skipped furiously when her gaze locked on Jake's heart-stalling smile. Sweet mercy, but she loved that smile! Was it any wonder she'd fallen for the man behind it?

Eric dragged her back to reality when he spoke. "Jake made bacon and eggs," he said. "I made the toast. We ate. But Jake said we had to wait to wake you up."

When he wound down, she sat up so Jake could place the tray across her knees. "How do you feel?"

Flustered by the caress in his voice, she told the truth. "A little sore. I mean...fine." Injuries aside, she hadn't felt this good in ages.

She inhaled deeply. "Everything smells wonderful. I can't believe how hungry I am." All her appetites had escaped restraint since she met this man.

Eric hopped on the bed and jostled her tray. "Eat, Mom. We don't want to miss the beginning of the movie."

Grabbing the glass of orange juice before it spilled, she took a sip. "That sounds like fun, but I've got to go to the office for a few hours this afternoon."

There was nothing pressing until her open house at four o'clock, but she desperately needed time to sort herself out. Her emotional equilibrium was iffy at best, and she couldn't afford to make a mistake now. Her love could destroy her this time but, even worse, it could hurt Jake or Eric. It was time to regain some semblance of control over her life, to think instead of feel her way through the decisions she could no longer avoid.

"You're not working today, Mom."

"Honey, we've gone over this before. I can't take time off whenever I want."

She glanced at Jake. "I wonder if all kids think their parents have the same vacation schedules they do."

He didn't automatically give her the support she'd learned to expect from him. "Eric," he said too many heartbeats later, "run downstairs and start on those dishes. I'll be down in a minute."

"Okie-dokie." Her son jumped off the bed with more enthusiasm than grace and dashed from the room.

Following him, Jake shut the bedroom door. Then he returned to stand beside the bed, his arms folded over his chest.

Carrie recognized the stance, his authoritative demeanor, and bit her bottom lip. Jake had only used this look a few times in her presence. Two weeks ago when Eric had talked back to her because she wouldn't let him go to the amusement park with some friends. Yesterday at the services picnic, when some older boys became too pushy with a group of teenaged girls. And, last night, when the harassed doctor and hospital nursing staff attempted to remove him from her examination room. Even the six-foot-six linebacker of a doctor had buckled under Jake's protective nature.

"About work," he began. "When I called Sam and told him you were hurt, he agreed you should stay off your feet. Take a day or two off and give yourself time to recover."

She choked down the coffee. A truckload of unresolved feelings, each scarier than the next, tipped over inside her. "A day or two? You and Sam decided? Who gave you the right to make my decisions for me?"

Jake raked a hand through his hair. "Last night—"

"Was last night! I might have lost my mind in the heat of the moment and fallen in love with you," she glared at him, "but I don't remember handing over control of my life."

"What are you talking about? I'm not trying to—" His arms dropped to his sides. "What did you say?"

"I don't remember handing over control of my life," she repeated. She'd lost that all on her own, but she was taking it back. Right now.

"Uh-uh." Jake shook his head, grinned. "You said you loved me."

Carrie replayed the conversation in her head. It didn't matter those weren't her exact words. The truth had inadvertently come out. There'd been no time to get used to her feelings, let alone decide what to do about them. "I just don't like anyone telling me what I can and cannot do," she said tightly. "I'm perfectly capable of getting out of this bed and going to work. There's nothing you can do to stop me."

The firm line of Jake's mouth testified to the control he had to exercise over his temper, but his tone was reasonable. "Fine," he said. "Get out of bed."

Carrie already regretted her irrational display, but no matter how much she cared about this man she needed her independence. It was the only protection she had against her vulnerability.

Taking a deep breath, she set aside the tray and tossed back the sheet. As if unaware she wore absolutely nothing but her determination, she eased to the side of the bed and set both feet on the floor. Defiantly, she pushed herself erect, and promptly cried out as agony burned up her leg.

Jake cursed as her ankle buckled. He caught her before she fell to the floor, swung her legs up, and laid her back on the bed. The sheet he threw over her nakedness virtually snapped with irritation. "That was a stupid thing to do!"

"Tell me something I don't know!" She sniffed at the tears of pain and mortification that ran down her cheeks unchecked.

A sob tore at her throat. She hated feeling helpless. Physically or emotionally. The last time she'd felt this powerless was the day she'd lost Eric's father. She'd sworn then to never depend on anyone for her happiness again. Now, look at her. She was a wreck.

Jake sat on the edge of the bed and rubbed both hands over the back of his neck. "The stupidity was mine," he said quietly. "I shouldn't have goaded you into trying that."

"Like I gave you a choice."

Wiping her tears with his fingertip, he smiled wryly. "Stubbornness is one of your less admirable qualities."

The tease underlying the accusation renewed some of her spunk. "Is that so? I don't remember being particularly obstinate before I met you."

"Then it's time someone shook all those nasty, bad habits out into the open."

"I don't know," she retorted. "That sounds kind of dangerous, like poking a stick at a grizzly bear."

His laughter filled the room and killed the rest of the tension between them. "Yeah. But think of the excitement."

She didn't need any more excitement. She already had Jake, who'd chosen that second to examine her injuries. His hand ran up and down the leg that wasn't covered by the sheet, from the sole of her foot to the top of her knee. On the return pass, he cupped a palm over her ankle. "This doesn't look any more swollen, but who knows how much more damage there is. Maybe we'd better get another x-ray."

A different kind of tension was forming and she couldn't let him see it with so many questions ripping at her peace of mind. "It's okay, *Doctor* Stefani," she said. "It hurts, but not any more than it did yesterday." A stretch of the truth, but the pain of standing on it was slowly dissipating.

Jake accepted her decision to avoid another nerve-wracking trip to the hospital, not necessarily because he agreed x-rays weren't needed, but because he had other things on his mind. What the hell just happened here?

When he entered the bedroom, he hadn't expected moonlight and roses, hot words and even hotter caresses. He'd been content to find the passion in Carrie's eyes, in her response to him despite Eric's presence. Then something happened and other emotions got in the way.

He'd made a mistake when he called Sam O'Reilly. His concern for Carrie's welfare was no excuse for going behind her back. She was a strong, independent woman. It was one of the things he loved about her. He should have consulted her. But that still didn't explain her extreme reaction. The only good thing that had come from her outburst was her slip about loving him.

"Honey, you're the only woman I know who declares her love, then throws a punch on the way out of the room."

"I didn't—"

"What? Tell me you love me or pick a fight with

me?" He'd waited forever to hear her utter three small words and, when he finally got them, she'd snatched them away.

"I didn't mean to do either." Her eyes filled. "I should have known you wouldn't leave it alone."

Jake caught a fresh tear on his thumb and felt like a monster. "Don't cry," he groaned. His lips caressed one damp eyelid, then the other. "I can't leave it alone. Don't you know all I want to do is love you?"

"Oh, Jake!"

He heard her confusion and addressed it the only way he knew how. He leaned over to kiss her, slowly, thoroughly, as he'd been dying to do since he walked into the room.

Carrie's mouth was hot and mobile under him. Their tongues mated. A taste. A quick touch. The fire below his belt became a critical threat to his sanity before he lifted his head. "Say it," he demanded, his breathing harsh and erratic. "Say 'I love you, Jake'."

"Yes, I do love you, Jake."

She could look happier about it. "I love you, too, honey," he said, slowly closing the gap between them. It was a chaste kiss, almost reverent but, too soon, it crashed out of bounds.

Without releasing her lips, he eased onto the bed to stretch down her length. When he guided her bare leg between his, she whimpered. He forgot their argument, intent only on Carrie's slender hands stroking with surety over his back, under his shirt. He trailed kisses over her skin, shaking so badly he could hardly think straight.

"No wonder I had to do all the dishes by myself!"

Jake registered Eric's disgruntled voice through a

white-hot haze of passion and tore his lips from Carrie's creamy skin. "I'm buying a lock for that door first chance I get," he muttered.

"What's the matter?" Carrie looked over his shoulder, then pushed weakly at his chest.

He refused to move until he had the sheet drawn over her nakedness, his body blocking his actions. When he sat up, he covered his lap with a corner of the sheet. "Eric." His voice cracked. "Your mother and I were—"

"Fooling around." Eric flushed, but his gaze held Jake's. "I'm almost nine. I'm not stupid."

The embarrassed moan behind him made Jake smile. Carrie could be proud of her son. He was smart as a whip and incredibly mature for his age. Less than a week ago at a friend's private lake, over a pair of fishing rods, Eric had asked Jake's intentions. Her own father couldn't have done better. "You've known for some time how I feel about your mom."

Eric grinned. "Yep." He turned to his mother. "Did you say yes, yet? 'Cause, if not, I can go get the popcorn ready for our movie. Jake has the extra-extra butter kind we like."

Carrie choked, her wits long since having deserted her. Jake had scrambled her brain so much before Eric walked into the room that it had only taken her son's blithe announcement about his knowledge of the birds and bees to finish the job.

"What am I supposed to say yes to?" Please let this request be a simple one, she silently begged.

"Whadda'ya think? I want Jake to be my dad, so you gotta marry him."

So much for easy requests. Her eyelids drifted down. Where was the air in this room?

Jake's gravelly voice reverberated above her head. "Thanks, Eric, but I'd rather do my own proposing, if you don't mind."

Her eyes popped open.

Wandering to the side of the bed, Eric peered down at her. "If you guys get married, Mom, I won't have to quit school when I'm sixteen. I kinda like going, and Jake says I have to go to college to be an astronaut."

"A backhanded endorsement if ever I heard one," Jake observed dryly. "Scram, kid, so your mom and I can talk."

Her son scrammed before Carrie could think of anything to say. Then the words came but they stuck to the roof of her mouth and she couldn't pry them loose. Jake was going to propose, if she didn't stop him.

"Where were we?" The smile on his lips matched the one in his eyes. He cupped her left hand in his palm and lifted her ring finger to his lips.

Panicked, she tugged at her hand. "Don't!"

Jake didn't let go. "Don't what, Carrie? This?" His mouth dropped to her wrist, right over her frantically beating pulse. "Or how about this?" He sucked the tender skin between her thumb and forefinger into his mouth. "Tell me what I'm not supposed to do, so I won't do it wrong."

Everything about the man felt too right. "Don't ask me to...sweet mercy, that feels so good."

She wished she dared give him everything he wanted, but if she didn't pull away now, he'd have the opportunity to form that question she wasn't prepared to face. "Jake, please! Eric could come back any minute."

He sighed heavily. "You know, he's a great kid, but we have to do something about his sense of timing." He kissed her knuckles. "Don't forget where we left off. We'll talk later."

Abruptly rolling off the bed, he grabbed her overnight bag from the dresser. "Go ahead and eat," he said, handing her the clothing Eric had packed. "When you're dressed, I'll carry you downstairs."

Carrie stared at his retreating figure and resisted the urge to call him back. She didn't trust herself not to ruin everyone's lives. It made good sense to separate herself from Jake for a while and, for that, she needed mobility. "Would you bring the crutches with you?"

He stopped in the open doorway to look at her. "They'll be difficult to manage on my stairs, but you can use them once we get you on safe ground. Okay?"

She nodded.

"Don't push too hard, too soon." He shifted his weight. "You will stay, won't you? I want to spend the last day of my vacation with you and Eric."

Carrie refused to think about his return to work tomorrow. "We'll stay until after dinner." But then, she was going home. One more night in Jake's bed and she'd never do what she had to do. She needed time to think about what that entailed.

"I guess that will give us enough time." His expression suddenly grew guarded. "There's something I need to tell you, but it'll wait until you're ready."

With one look at his face, she knew his news would up the emotional stakes and compound her dilemma. It'd wait, all right. She wasn't laying odds that she'd ever be ready.

Chapter Thirteen

"You owe me two thousand dollars!" Eric's grin was gleeful as he pointed at the plastic hotel on the game board centered on the living room coffee table. "That property's mine."

Jake sighed. This was the longest game in history when a man had more important things on his mind. He had an hour or two, at most, if dinner was delayed before Carrie sailed out his front door on her crutches.

He waved one property card and his last five-dollar bill in the air. "This is it. I'm busted."

Lounging on the couch with her foot up, Carrie gestured to her own wad of phony cash. "I could lend you more money."

He'd be happier with more of her time. Like a lifetime. If he didn't know better, he'd think she'd deliberately thrown a distance between them since he carried her downstairs. She'd accepted the circumstances of her husband's death, faced down a city park filled with his fellow officers, and revealed her feelings for him. Her perceptions about his job had changed. She loved him despite his uniform.

He hadn't told her about his S.W.A.T. detail yet, but it shouldn't make a difference now. He was hopeful their relationship could weather his career choices, whatever those choices might be once he spoke to his uncle tomorrow. So why did he feel like he'd run into a blind alley with no ammunition and no back up?

"Thanks," he said, rising from his seat, "but I know when I'm beat. You two can fight it out while I feed Riker and order the pizza."

He'd taken two steps toward the kitchen when someone leaned on the doorbell. He growled when he finally reached the front door and jerked it open. "What?"

Ramón almost fell into the entry juggling a volleyball, a net, an overflowing bat bag, and a stack of casserole dishes. "Hey, partner. Take something before I hurt myself."

Grabbing the nearest casseroles, Jake looked over Ramón's head at Maria. "What is all this?"

She adjusted her own armload, reached around her husband to catch a glass-domed lid slipping off his stack, and tucked it between the tablecloths she carried. "We promised the kids dinner and a movie, and thought we'd drop these things on our way. You left everything behind when you rushed Carrie to the hospital yesterday. Remember?"

Jake hadn't given a thought to any of it. "Thanks. The city athletic department will have my hide if I don't get their equipment back by Wednesday. Everything else came from the senior center."

He glanced toward the street in time to see the Herrera van bounce on its springs, grateful the clan wasn't inclined to stay. As much as he liked the enthusiastic bunch, he wasn't ready to entertain them tonight.

"Maria!   Ramón!" Carrie's voice preceded the

thump of her crutches on the entry floor. "I didn't know you were coming to dinner."

Jake only muttered one Italian word under his breath, but it was one with which his partner was familiar. His gaze sharpened. "Uh, we were just explaining that we—"

Carrie came to a halt beside Jake and looked up at him. "We can order a bigger pizza, can't we?"

Did she have to look so happy to see his friends? "Sure," he said then turned to his partner. "I've unpacked my DVD and Blue-ray box, too. There's bound to be something the kids haven't seen."

"We were thinking about pizza anyway." Ramón lifted one eyebrow, giving him one last opportunity to change his mind.

He kissed the chance good-bye with a wave at the car. He grinned when four kids tumbled out. If he knew Ramón's children, it would be hours before things settled down again. He'd just guaranteed Carrie wouldn't be hopping out the door any time soon. It was good enough for now.

~~~

Surreptitiously checking her watch, Carrie frowned. What happened to her plan to leave after dinner? The strain of keeping Jake at arm's length had eased since Ramón and Maria arrived with their kids, but she was still strung tighter than piano wire.

She could chalk that up to the way everyone sat in the living room after the kids ran outside to play. The Herrera's had each taken an armchair, leaving Jake and Carrie the couch. She was initially relieved when he sat at the opposite end so she could keep her ankle elevated on a pillow, but then he lifted her pillow and ankle into his lap. For the past hour they'd been talking, Jake had absently stroked his hand over her ankle and up her leg.

It felt too good to have his hands on her. Chatting with his friends while the kids played in the backyard with the dog felt too natural, too. She had to get out of there before she found herself alone with him again, before she had to face the question she saw in his eyes whenever he looked at her. She was opting for later. Much later.

A ready excuse formed in her mind. Eric had to get to bed at a decent hour or he'd be a bear when she dropped him off at the babysitter's house on her way to the office in the morning. He was already upset about having to go to a "real" babysitter now that Jake's return to work was imminent. The only thing preventing her son's mutiny thus far was the knowledge his trip to Florida to visit Tomás's parents was less than a week away.

Carrie listened as Ramón finished another story about growing up as one of six rambunctious kids. Evidently his youngest brother broke his leg in a fall from a riser of bleachers while mooning the members of his high school graduating class.

"Of course," he said with a chuckle, "Luis is almost out of law school now so he should be past that stage." He made a face at Maria. "On second thought, maybe we'll miss his graduation next spring."

When the general laughter trailed off, Carrie took advantage of the lull in conversation to put her plan in motion. She lifted her leg off Jake's lap, stood on one foot, and jockeyed her crutches into place under her arms. "Eric and I need to go soon," she said to Maria. "Let's pull those root beer floats together before it's too late."

"I can help Maria." Jake stood. "You should sit."

"I need to move."

He frowned at her, but finally turned away with a nod to Ramón.

While the men went outside to round up the children, the two women entered the kitchen. Maria scooped vanilla ice cream into tall glasses. Carrie opened the two jugs of soda on the counter. She hesitated before gathering the nerve to ask the question that had plagued her since the picnic. "Maria, how do you all do it?"

"You just pour the root beer over the ice cream."

"I'm not talking about the floats."

Maria glanced up from her task and groaned. "Don't say it! When we stayed tonight, your evening was ruined. I told Ramón the last thing you two needed was a couple of old married people and their kids busting in."

"You didn't ruin anything. I'm glad you came. I need to talk to you."

"About what?"

All of a sudden, she was grateful her departure was postponed. Maria was the one person who might understand her predicament. Leaning against the counter, her crutches set aside, Carrie carefully chose her words. "You're married to a policeman. Several of your in-laws are cops. Do you worry about them?"

Maria laughed. "Good heavens, yes. Don't you worry about the people you love?"

"Of course, I do, but that's different."

Filling the last glass, she set the scoop on the counter and licked melted ice cream from her fingertips. "I'm getting the distinct impression your question isn't as simple as it sounds." She studied Carrie's face. "This is about Jake, isn't it? I was right. You do care for him."

"I'm desperately in love with the man," she admitted, "but just thinking about the dangers of his job, of losing him, terrifies me."

"You think you'd worry about him less if he was a bus driver or an insurance salesman?"

She nodded, even though she knew it wasn't necessarily true. Tomás was an insurance broker. It hadn't protected him. But, it wasn't as if he'd deliberately walked into the bank on that day six years earlier expecting danger either. Jake walked into potentially dangerous situations every day. It was that thought which made her heart tremble. She'd lost too many people in her life.

"Look, Carrie, you can't separate the man from his profession, especially not in this case.

"Jake is like Ramón. His job is an integral part of who he is inside," she tapped her fist against her chest in demonstration, "even if he does work hard to keep his personal and professional lives separate. When he puts on his uniform, it's like he turns on a light switch. He needs a different attitude to meet the demands of his job. But remove that uniform? The man is the same underneath. It's the man you fell in love with, not his job, that's important."

Carrie dragged her hands through her hair. "I understand that. But it doesn't tell me how to cope with it, how to make it work."

"If you're looking for easy answers, you won't find them. Some people merely shut the dangers from their mind. Some worry themselves and their families sick."

Maria shook her head. "I won't kid you. The divorce rate is high in police work. You must make peace with this or you're doomed from the start."

She wasn't hearing anything new, but she'd hoped for more. "What do you do?"

"Accept it." She shrugged. "I know the hazards of Ramón's job, but I can't dwell on them. When he walks out the door, he's a man going to work. He's not a man going to work in a uniform."

"I'm not sure—"

"Make sure! If you love Jake as much as you say, you have to love all of him, not just the parts you can handle. You have to have faith in his ability to take care of himself out there and, God forbid, something does happen you will have his love until then. That man will be in it for the long haul."

The sound of voices nearing the back door warned Carrie that Jake, Ramón, and the children would soon be joining them. Her heart flipped over. "What if I can't do that?"

"Then, you have no business breaking that man's heart." Maria fixed her with a stare. "I love Jake like my own brother. If you can't love him the way he deserves, let him find someone who can. Get out of his life and don't look back."

Carrie didn't think she could do that either now she knew how she felt about Jake. Had falling in love changed everything or nothing? She was running out of time to figure it out.

~~~

Jake walked through the kitchen door with the youngest of Ramón's brood riding piggyback, her tiny, bare feet kicking her "horsy" mercilessly. "Whoa, partner," he said with a groan of mock pain. "This old horse can't go any faster."

Ramón peeled the three-year-old from Jake's back. "Come here, Calamity Jane," he said. "We'll find you a younger horsy." With a chuckle, he tossed her onto his shoulders. The child promptly dug both hands into her father's hair and renewed her bucking.

Since Jake and his friend were barely three weeks apart in age, he laughed. "Tell me when you've paid enough for that crack about my age, partner, and I might save you."

A yelp of surprise was Ramón's response when his rider almost bucked herself off her perch at the same time a beeping sound filled the kitchen.

Carrie frowned when the room went silent. "What was that?"

Quickly handing the little girl off to her mother, Ramón yanked a device from his pocket. "My pager," he explained, lifting it to look at the number on the screen.

Jake's pulse had speeded up in the last few seconds, an automatic response honed by a year of carrying his own beeper. Everyone on the S.W.A.T. team had one, although Jake had turned his off at the start of his vacation. He just realized it was the one aspect of his job he hadn't thought he'd miss. "Grab the phone in the living room," he suggested.

Standing in the doorway, he listened to Ramón's half of the conversation with one ear and the conversation that had resumed in the kitchen with the other. He wanted to kiss Maria for defusing the situation. The baby perched on her hip, she'd begun directing the root beer pouring operations, leaving

Carrie too busy mixing floats to question the vibrating tension in the air.

He leaned into the doorjamb and enjoyed the tantalizing view of her curved backside swaying back and forth as she added foaming soda to each glass. He'd begun to foam inside, too, at the thought of other creative uses for ice cream and root beer when Ramón came up behind him.

"False alarm," he said, his voice lowered. "Myers was looking for some equipment."

Jake chuckled at the thought of Leon Myers, the S.W.A.T. ordnance handler. "Myers needs a life," he shot over his shoulder.

"Everyone was saying the same thing about you until a month ago."

Turning his back to the kitchen, Jake defended himself. "I'm not that bad."

Ramón snorted. "No, buddy, you're worse. I wasn't sure why you bought this house when you spend every waking hour at the station."

He hesitated, then shook his head. "I'd better warn you now. Captain Monroe's made some noises about pulling you off S.W.A.T. detail, although I think it's just talk because you're family. He's still having kittens about that junkie nearly taking your head off, even though everyone knows you responded appropriately."

"Yeah, I was lucky the incident didn't earn me a trip to the morgue instead of a month's vacation." He trailed off when he registered the heat of someone behind him. There was only one person he didn't want to see right then.

With a deep breath, he turned to find Carrie in front of him, leaning hard on one crutch as if it was all that held her up. His heart lurched at the look of betrayal on her face. He tried to brazen it out. "Is that for me?" he asked, indicating the root beer float she held in her free hand.

Without a word, she thrust the glass forward and pushed past him. Jake was left with the sound of her shuffling gait disappearing behind him and most of the contents of the glass dripping down his front.

Seven pairs of eyes, reflecting either confusion or surprise, stared at Jake. Ramón was the first to speak. "She didn't know?"

Jake shook his head. "I was going to tell her tonight."

Maria groaned. "Oh, Jake, you don't know what you've done. Go after her!"

After a quick glance at Eric, Jake left the room. By the time he reached Carrie she was tugging ineffectually at the front door, obviously blinded by the tears streaming down her cheeks. Feeling like a jerk, he placed both hands on the door around her. "Carrie, don't go," he said into her hair. "I can explain."

She pivoted on one heel, her crutch cracking him in the shin. "I don't want your explanations. I just want to go home."

Jake's temper flared. "We need to talk this out. Even criminals get a fair trial in this country."

"So talk," she said mutinously, her hand clenched tight on the crutch.

When she swayed back against the door for additional support, he cursed under his breath. In one smooth movement he swept her up, crutch and all, in his arms. He'd carried her halfway up the stairs before she opened her mouth. "Not one word," he said tightly, "until we get some privacy."

She subsided with a glare, her lips pursed.

He carried her into his bedroom and sat her down on the edge of the bed. Then, he shut the door and leaned against it, his arms crossed over his chest. "Okay, now we talk."

Carrie laid her crutch on the bed within reach and simply sat there without saying anything. Beginning to feel the cold seeping into his skin from his ruined shirt, he stepped further into the room and yanked it over his head. He threw it toward the chair in the corner and grabbed another one from the closet. "You can stop looking at me that way. I'm not going to bite." He jammed first one arm, then another, into the clean shirt.

Absently registering the sound of ripping material, Carrie was distracted by the ripple of his tight abs. She should feel intimidated, but wasn't. She knew Jake too well. His arms might have been tense under her legs and shoulders when he carried her upstairs, his dark eyes shooting armor-piercing bullets, but he'd set her down gently, almost delicately. He was a protective man through and through. It was one of the things she loved about him.

Self-preservation called for an immediate retreat, but she felt her resolve softening. "When were you going to tell me?"

"Not until our fiftieth wedding anniversary?" He sighed when she didn't smile. "What do you want me to say, Carrie? I wanted to tell you, but you weren't prepared to discuss my job in any way."

All her insecurities threatened to escape her grasp. "Who says I want to discuss it now?"

Jake scowled and reopened the closet door. Silently,

he drew out a crisply starched, blue uniform and tossed it on the bed beside her.

His masculine scent stirred the air and invaded her lungs before her defenses could snap into place. Reluctant to release even that small part of him, she held her breath and examined the metal badge pinned to his shirt. Her fingers traced the rough surface that had lain over Jake's heart the past nine years.

Lucky thing.

"It still comes down to that, doesn't it?"

Carrie snatched her hand into her lap. "What?"

"My badge. My uniform. I'm still a member of that terrible fraternity responsible for Tomás's death."

"Yes." She blinked. "I mean, no."

"Which is it? Yes or no?"

Honesty compelled her to answer part of the question. "You know I don't hold the police responsible for Tomás's death anymore." She rose unsteadily to stand on her one good ankle. Despite a slight swaying motion, she felt more in control. "Look, Jake, I'm not ready to discuss this."

"Tough."

The sharp word lifted her chin. "Excuse me?"

"You might not want to have this discussion, but we can't walk away from it now. We agreed our jobs were off the table until I returned to work, that we'd explore what we felt about each other. I'm returning to work tomorrow." His eyes narrowed. "You don't deny this is about my uniform. Are you afraid of me, of what I do?"

"No! I see the way you are with Eric, with other people, with me. I might not have seen you on the job, but I'm sure you're tough when it's required and compassionate when your work allows for it." She was weakening, but didn't know what to do about it. "And beneath your sometimes aggravating over-protectiveness is sensitivity and a supportive nature. I'd never have fallen in love with you if I was afraid of you."

Jake studied her, as if trying to decipher a particularly intricate puzzle. "Then what has you running scared?"

Carrie tousled her hair with her fingers. There had to be a way to make him understand her jumbled feelings. "I promised myself I wouldn't risk...I'm not strong enough to deal with..."

"Go on." He walked toward her slowly, watching her like he expected her to bolt any second. "What can't you risk? Your heart? You already gave it to me." He paused. "As for your strength, you're the strongest woman I know. You don't just taste life. You experience it."

The bed pressed against the back of her knees. "If that's what you think, you don't know me very well. I'm no risk-taker."

"Yeah?" He looked skeptical. "The woman I know wears bright colors and seeks new food sensations. She's made a career for herself in a real estate market that's nothing short of frightening."

He ran a fingertip down her cheek. "The woman I know allowed me into her life, despite a poor history with her own family and an even worse one with cops. She makes love like there's no tomorrow and stands up under everything I dish out."

His lips twitched into a ghost of a smile. "It's your strength and independence that makes me want you, even if they do frustrate the hell out of me sometimes."

She hobbled along the edge of the bed, seeking

distance on the opposite side, but Jake followed her. "Will you stop stalking me?" she cried.

A muscle jumped in his cheek, but he took a step back. "Not until I deal with whatever's bothering you."

"You're not dealing with anything. I am. This," she waved a hand between them, "we are a disaster waiting to happen." She reached out and tried to push him back another step.

Jake wouldn't budge. "Do you want to clarify that last statement?"

No! It hurt too much to think about never seeing Jake again. Never feel his touch. "I can't breathe," she whispered, gulping for air.

He moved away to the center of the room and tunneled his hands into his pockets. "Well?"

Her thoughts were chaotic, but one stood out. Stark. Terrifying. Inescapable. "Jake, what you do is dangerous. I-I'm scared to death of losing you. It was bad enough before, when I thought you were just a cop. But, S.W.A.T? It's too much."

The silence in the bedroom was oppressive. Carrie felt like she'd been dragged through an emotional shredder. She stared at the floor, sure her heart had to be down there somewhere, mangled beyond recognition.

"You're denying our future because you're sure some faceless danger is lurking around the corner waiting to rip it apart."

"I have to protect myself. Protect Eric," she said, defensive under his censure.

Turning abruptly, Jake made his way back to the closet. His hands were full when he returned to her side. One item at a time, he threw his baton, handcuffs, Mace, and bulletproof vest on top of his uniform. He carefully set his gun on the pillow at the head of the pile.

"Honey," he said, "these cover most contingencies. I also have a lot of special training and experience under my belt. When I go out on a S.W.A.T. call, I have even more stringent protection and equipment. My training is constantly upgraded. My physical safety is as tight as I can make it."

She examined the items littering the bed and felt a chill creeping into her soul. "I heard what Ramón said about the junkie. You were almost killed."

"You want me to quit S.W.A.T.? Quit being a cop? What?"

"No. I'd never ask that," she said, not sure how to make him understand. "Your work is part of you. But it doesn't change the fact you can't promise me forever. You can't promise you'll never die." She'd lost too many loved ones. If she lost Jake, too, it would kill her. Her eyes filled, overflowed.

Jake looked like he'd been poleaxed. "That's quite a hole you've dug for yourself. You can't promise any of those things either, but I'm willing to bet we can have fifty or sixty great years."

Palm behind her neck, he drew her to him so she could feel the heat of his body. "Life doesn't come with money-back guarantees, sweetheart. You take the good with the bad. Hiding from emotional hazards isn't protection. It's denial. Of everything you can be, everything you can have."

"What's your point?"

"The point is you quit before you start. Maybe you aren't as strong as I thought. If I've made a mistake, I apologize."

He stepped back. His hand dropped to his side. "I need the woman I love to walk beside me, not behind me." His tone brooked no argument. "She has to meet life's obstacles head on. When I come home from a day of solving other people's problems, I don't want more problems. I need a mate, a partner. Someone who will give me the same love and support I'll give her, no matter where our careers take us. No matter what life throws at us."

"Jake—"

"I'm not finished," he interrupted harshly. "I love you, Carrie. I want to marry you and have a house full of children just like Eric. But you've got to meet the challenges with me, give it everything you've got, because I can't settle for anything less than a lifetime."

He raised a hand to touch her again, but didn't complete the action. "I'm ready for that kind of love. If you aren't willing to take that first step out into the open with me, then you aren't the woman I thought you were and we have nothing more to talk about."

Anguish tore at her insides. "Please, Jake, maybe in time—"

"You've had enough time." His jaw was hard, his eyes unreadable. "You need to make a decision."

So many conflicting emotions were tearing at her insides, but she reined them in and straightened her backbone before she broke her own heart. "Then, no. I can't do this."

"Would it make a difference if I did leave S.W.A.T.?"

She wanted to say yes, but this wasn't about what he did or didn't do with his career. It was about her fear that she couldn't survive losing him. "It's too late," she whispered. "Goodbye, Jake."

The quiet, broken words were shocking enough to numb, yet pain slashed through her. Calling on every last ounce of willpower she had, she forced herself to pick up her crutch from the bed, hop out of the room and down the stairs where she found Eric standing next to Maria.

"Carrie—"

"I'm sorry, Maria. You were right." She took a deep breath when Ramón approached her with her other crutch. Carrie tucked it under her free arm, then looked into his eyes. "Ramón, I-I...just take care of him. Please?"

He nodded.

Before she could fall completely apart, she had Eric open Jake's door for the last time and they walked in silence to their side of the street. Her heart, she left behind on Jake's bedroom floor.

Chapter Fourteen

Eric eyed Carrie over his cereal four days later, his hand clenched around his spoon. "Moom, if I don't go this morning, it'll be too late!"

Unable to contend with his confusion and hurt, Carrie swung around on her crutches and began to prepare tea. She mumbled a curse when she splashed boiling water on her hand. "Eric, stop! You can't go to Jake's to remind him about this afternoon, and that's final."

Her crutches crashed to the floor as she shuffled to the freezer for an ice cube to rub over her angry, red skin. This was Jake's fault. If he hadn't promised to see Eric off to his grandparents in Florida today, none of this would be happening. Eric wouldn't be upset. Her hand wouldn't need a skin graft. She wouldn't be so blasted close to tears.

Blinking back her self-pity, she stared at the melting ice. The truth is she'd have to face Jake sooner or later since they lived on the same street, but today, right now, was a no-win proposition. She was still too miserable. Too vulnerable.

"But he might forget if I don't remind him."

Carrie dabbed a dish towel against her dripping hand. "So, he'll forget. What do you want me to do?"

A tear fell down her son's cheek, followed swiftly by a torrent. He thrust away from the kitchen table. "You're so mean," he wailed, dashing from the room. His sobs rang out until a door slammed upstairs and cut them off.

Bewildered, she stared at his empty chair and the pool of milk skimming rapidly across the table from his tipped glass. She dropped onto a stool and watched the liquid slip off the edge of the table to the floor. The steady drizzle slowed to an occasional drip. She didn't wipe up the mess. Her whole life was a mess. What was a little spilt milk?

Why did Jake have to force an ultimatum on her? Until he'd knocked on her door and blithely walked into her heart, she hadn't known how empty her life had become. He'd breathed life into her soul, filled her heart with love, and she missed him so much.

She'd tried to push him into a convenient mental closet, but he pursued her through her long days. When she crawled into bed at night, he crawled in with her. In the darkness locks came undone, closets opened, and a multitude of memories and unfulfilled dreams spilled out. Each morning, the ache inside her became more unbearable.

When she'd left Jake's house four days ago swearing to forget him, she hadn't counted on the effect it would have on Eric either. Cutting herself off from the man she loved was bound to be painful, but this trauma, this abysmal sense of loss, the increasing dissension between her and Eric was awful. She'd ripped the man he loved like a father from his life and he was devastated.

It had to stop.

She pushed to her feet and hopped across the

kitchen to pick up her crutches. Looking down at them, she abandoned them where they lay. It was time to stand on her own two feet again.

Gingerly working her way upstairs, she knocked on her son's bedroom door and entered the room. "Eric?"

With a loud sniff, he flipped over on his single bed facing its twin where his friends slept during sleepovers.

His rejection hit her like a physical blow. Sitting next to him, she placed a tremulous hand on his back, hunched beneath his Colorado Rockies T-shirt. "Honey, please talk to me. I'm sorry I yelled at you."

Eric turned over. "Me, too," he said. "I didn't mean what I said, that you were mean, I mean."

Carrie smoothed his hair off his forehead, love for him reminding her of what was important. "I've been awfully grouchy lately, and it really isn't your fault. I'm supposed to be the grownup here. Forgive me?"

He nodded. "You're mad at Jake, huh? You're mad because he didn't tell you about S.W.A.T. That's why I can't go over there anymore."

She didn't want to think about the night she'd walked away from Jake's love. "You heard everything?"

"You were talking pretty loud." He ducked his head. "I was outside the door listening until Mrs. Herrera came and got me. I'm sorry."

That explained why he was standing at the bottom of the stairs with Maria. As sick as she felt about what happened, what Eric had heard, she didn't have the heart to chastise him for eavesdropping. "If I'm mad at anyone, it's with myself," she said with a shrug. "Sometimes, grownups don't always do the right thing."

That hadn't come out quite the way she intended.

What did she regret? Falling in love or walking away? If Jake hadn't pushed, if he'd given her more time to analyze her new feelings, would her answer have been the same? "Eric, to tell the truth, I don't know what I feel right now."

His chin dropped as he picked at the edge of his NFL bedspread. "Jake isn't going to be my dad, is he?"

Right or wrong, she'd answered Jake's ultimatum. She drew in a long, shaky breath that did nothing to loosen the hard knot in her chest. "No, Eric."

"Don't you like him anymore?"

Unable to escape the question in his pain-filled eyes, she rose from the bed. "I love Jake, honey, but sometimes other feelings get in the way. I can't marry someone just to give you the dad you want. Understand?"

"I guess." He finished in a mumble. "But I still don't see why I can't go over to Jake's house."

It was a huge mistake to cut Eric off from Jake. She could see that now. Her son had never known the love of his father. He'd been too young when Tomás died to remember much about him, and she sure hadn't helped by not talking about his father as he grew up. He'd had Davy and Sam to do guy things, but Jake was the first man to freely take on all of her son's needs. Her fears had stolen even that small pleasure from him.

Eric needed Jake as much as she suspected Jake needed Eric. Her problems had to be separated from their relationship. No matter how much it hurt. "Go tell Jake we're leaving for the airport at four o'clock."

A quick grin wiped away Eric's gloomy expression. "You mean it?"

She rallied a bright smile. "Sure. Go ahead. If you've

missed him, you can leave a note on his door."

Eric jumped from the bed and kissed her cheek. "Thanks, Mom. You're the best!" Then he rushed from the room, leaving her with another gaping hole in her heart and an unbelievable desolation gnawing on her soul.

~~~

Eric surreptitiously wiped moisture off his cheeks, his gaze fixed on Jake's house through the back seat window of Carrie's car. "He's not coming."

Guilt piled a little higher on her shoulders as she fiddled once more with the placement of her son's suitcases on the seat next to him. She should have called Jake at the station, if necessary, to remind him about Eric's departure. "We can wait a few more minutes, honey," she said. "He'll come."

It was all too likely he'd never want to see *her* again. He'd never deliberately hurt Eric. She whispered a plea. "Hurry, Jake."

As if conjured from thin air, he was there. Her pulse leaped when a Riverton police car rounded the corner of their street and stopped in front of her driveway. Ramón waved to her from the driver's side as Jake climbed out of the car in his uniform, huge, powerful, and so sexy her heart pounded for another reason. The scowl on his face melted into his trademark come-and-get-me smile when he looked into her eyes. For that instant, nothing stood between them—not his job, his uniform, nor her deeply-entrenched fears—and she felt his warmth and love wrap around her, hold her.

Eric shattered the illusion, launching himself out of the car and down the drive to throw his arms around Jake's waist. "You came!"

"Sorry I'm late," he said to her over Eric's head, his smile fading. "I'm on day shift now. We're between calls."

The weight of his cool appraisal chilled her insides. She must have imagined the light of love in his eyes because it wasn't there now. His professional mask was firmly in place. "It's okay. The plane's departure was pushed back an hour." She glanced at her watch. "We still have a few minutes before we have to leave."

"I don't want to go to Florida, Mom. I want to stay here with Jake." Eric buried his face in the front of his uniform.

At a loss for words, she glanced at Jake. She was startled to see how tired he looked at that moment. There were new lines around his eyes and his face looked sharper somehow, like he'd lost weight. He studied her face, too, until the silence between them grew taut. For one crazy minute, she wondered if he could see her regret and her unbearable need to retract their last argument. Then, he looked away.

Jake peeled Eric away and hunkered down until they were at eye level. "Son, your grandparents are looking forward to your visit. It wouldn't be fair to disappoint them now, would it?"

Eric shook his head. "I guess not."

"You've been talking about exploring the Florida Keys with Grandma and Grandpa Padilla for weeks. You're going to have a great time fishing on the boat. Just don't forget to take pictures for me so I can see all the whoppers you catch."

"I'll take lots and lots."

Carrie couldn't stem her tears when Jake hugged Eric before rising to his feet. No matter how badly she'd hurt him, the man could still give her son what he needed. She wished she could walk into his arms and tell him how much she loved him. How much she'd always love him. "Jake?"

As if he sensed her vulnerability, how tempted she was to throwing caution to the wind, he moved toward her and brushed her tears away. "We'll talk," he said in a low voice meant only for her. "There are things I need to tell yo—"

A noise cut him off, and she jerked back. It didn't take her long to identify the beeping sound came from Jake. He had a pager identical to the one Ramón had worn the other night attached to his black leather belt. She stared at it like it was a coiled snake, ready to strike, her heart pumping madly in counterpoint to the beeps.

Jake said something in Italian that sounded like a curse word before he yanked the device from his belt to read the number.

"I've got it," Ramón said from the car.

He replaced the device on his belt and ruffled Eric's hair with one hand. "Take care of yourself, Eric, and we'll talk when you get back."

Her son nodded.

A burst of radio chatter filled the air. "Wrap it up, Stefani," Ramón called out. "We've got to go."

When Jake looked at her, Carrie's throat seized upon a knot of raw emotions. Anger and hurt. Yearning and sadness. Love, the kind that would fill her heart forever if only she'd let it. She didn't know how to push the words into the open.

Evidently, Jake didn't either. He reached out a strong hand, cupped it around the back of her neck, and kissed her. His lips were a soft brush against hers. Then, he turned away.

Numb, Carrie watched him climb into the police car. He'd barely settled before Ramón kicked on their lights and siren, and they were gone. She wanted to run after Jake, stop him. She had to let him go.

She didn't know how long she stood there in the driveway before Eric tugged on her arm. "Mom?"

"We'll have to hurry to make your plane," she said, her voice amazingly calm as she led her son back to the car.

The drive to Denver International Airport in the middle of rush hour traffic took longer than she expected, but at least she had something to occupy her brain. She parked in a short term airport lot, rode the train with Eric to the proper concourse, and managed to arrive at the departure gate with time to spare. Carrie was glad she'd made arrangements ahead of time to escort her son to his plane instead of simply handing him over to an attendant at the security gate, but now she was here with nothing to do but fuss over Eric. All she could think about was Jake and where he was headed.

She knew it was a S.W.A.T. call because it came from Jake's beeper, not the police car radio. He was rushing to a crime scene that demanded his special training. Was it a gunman threatening a school or mall? A bank robbery with hostages like the one that had taken Eric's father? Past mingled with present until she couldn't separate the two. The chaos of blue uniforms and flashing lights, fear twisting her insides, the agony of losing a loved one.

"Jeez, Mom, let go! I'll do it myself."

She looked down to see she'd tucked Eric's shirt into

his jeans like he was a two-year-old again. "I'm sorry, honey." She took the nearest seat, her hands folded in her lap against her need to push back a stray hair on his forehead. *You can't fall apart until after you put Eric on the plane.*

"He'll be okay, Mom."

Carrie stared at her son's confident expression, so reminiscent of Jake's, and felt something unravel. "You don't know any such thing."

"Sure, I do. Jake's good. He's got awards and stuff. He's got tons of gear to wear, too. He showed me when I asked him."

"So you were worried, too."

"Yeah, a little," he said with a shrug, "but not anymore."

Where did her son find such blind faith? "Eric, things still happen. Do you have any idea how hard it is to lose someone you love?"

"Well, no." He hesitated, frowned. "Does that mean you wouldn't have married my Dad if you knew he was going to die?"

The question jolted her. "Of course not. I loved your father. Honey, if I hadn't married him, I wouldn't have you. I love you very much."

"Do you love Jake as much as Dad?"

"Yes," she said, although she hated to admit that what she felt for Jake was so much more than what she'd had with Tomás. She'd been too young and naive to appreciate the depths love could reach.

"What's the difference?"

Her head came up. She'd missed something. "What?"

Eric exhaled heavily, like he was talking to a

hardheaded child. "What's the difference between Dad and Jake?"

There were a number of differences between the two men, but that wasn't what Eric wanted to know. Carrie ran her fingers through her hair, unsettled. Sometimes she wondered if an eighty-year-old man inhabited her son's eight-year-old body. Where did he get these mature notions?

Carrie heard the flight attendant call out boarding instructions. "Listen, Eric, that's you. You've got to go. We'll discuss this when you get back."

"But--"

She hugged him fiercely. "Say hi to Grandma and Grandpa for me. Have them call me the second they pick you up, okay?" When he nodded, she stroked a hand down his cheek one last time and handed him over to a smiling attendant.

With a wave, Eric disappeared down the gangway with his companion. Left with nothing but an overwhelming loneliness to accompany her, she blindly watched the plane taxi away. Only then did she go back to her car and drive away from the airport toward home.

Only, home wasn't where she ended up.

Somehow, she found herself pulling into an empty parking lot near the address she'd heard over the police radio before Jake and Ramón drove off earlier that afternoon. She stared at the crowd gathered outside the perimeter barricades that had been erected to keep bystanders safe.

Gulping air into her lungs, she recognized the wild surge of panic. This was nuts. Jake would have a fit if he knew what she was doing.

What are you doing?

Calm slid over her as she realized she knew exactly why she was there. She had to confront the last of her demons, the memories, to see if she could live with the past and build a new future. If she failed, no one needed to know. If she succeeded, well, she owed it to herself and Eric and Jake to find out if she'd made the worst mistake of her adult life.

Getting out of the car, she joined the small crowd standing directly behind the line of barriers. She absorbed the sounds around her. The quietly spoken directions of the men and women in uniforms. The equally quiet, tense words several reporters spoke in front of television cameras. She couldn't hear what they were saying, but that was probably a good thing. She wasn't sure she could handle any more details right now.

She searched the faces nearby, even knowing it was unlikely she'd see Jake. She'd watched enough movies and news reports to know there was probably a S.W.A.T. truck somewhere out of sight, where orders were given, preparations made. Preparations designed to save innocent lives should negotiations fail. As they'd failed six years ago.

Through an extraordinary sequence of events, she'd lost Tomás. But, it was no one's fault. She accepted that, was grateful sixteen additional bank employees and hostages had survived, that Stan Murcheson had lived. He and the others could just as easily have died or been injured.

Jake was right. There were no guarantees. Too many things could go wrong. Amazingly enough, it wasn't the possibility of Jake's death that had plagued her the most these past few days, but his life. Was he eating right?

Was he working too hard? Did he smile today? How did she think she could let him face a serious illness or debilitating injury alone? She couldn't tear herself away when he had the flu, for goodness sake.

Maria had told Carrie to have faith in Jake. She did. It was herself in which she had little faith. Life held more risks than death. She'd survived loss before and could do it again. She was a strong, mature woman, not a frightened, inexperienced young girl. She needed to trust her instincts. They'd been screaming for weeks there was nothing more right than loving Jake.

Her breath caught on the burning truth. She *had* made the worst mistake of her life. The question was what was she going to do about it?

~~~

Something's wrong.

The feeling was fuzzy around the edges, but it was enough to drag Jake from a deep sleep. Fighting for his usual alertness, he pried his gritty eyelids open and listened to the muted night sounds. Riker wasn't barking a warning from the other room where he'd curled up every night since Eric last slept there.

Had he actually heard something or was fatigue playing tricks on his mind? The ping of something against the window glass swiftly answered the question.

Tumbling out of bed into his cutoffs, he groaned as he glanced at the clock on his way out of the room. Four a.m. It had taken most of the night to break away from the station after the shooting incident that had torn him away from Carrie and Eric yesterday. He'd barely closed his eyes. A prowler was the last thing he needed. He hoped the perp in the back yard was ready to get his arms ripped off!

On bare feet, Jake ran down the stairs with Riker, who whined when he uttered a single command to guard the house. Then he eased out the front door with nothing in his hands, but a desire to mete out punishment. It was only as he peered around the corner of the house at the gate leading to the backyard that he remembered an earlier incident. Was it only a month ago?

His bare toes curled into the cold, damp lawn as the memory rushed over him. His exhaustion after coming in from that dogwatch. The same sense of intrusion. The veiling, morning fog drifting off the river. The gaping gate. Everything was the same.

Everything, that is, except him.

That was the morning he'd captured a small boy with a camera around his neck. *Eric.* It was the morning that same boy's mother captured Jake's heart. *Carrie.* He leaned against the side of the house, his chest tight. It had taken only one luscious woman and a skinny would-be vandal to change his life forever. He refused to let either of them go. Today, he'd convince Carrie if he had to lock her up to do it.

The discordant sound of shattering glass broke his immobility. "Get it in gear, Stefani," he admonished. "That's not Eric back there this time." His heart briefly winged its way to Florida, his thoughts ran upstairs to his forgotten revolver, while his bare feet took the rest of him into the gray morning mist.

"Umpf." Jake rammed his shoulder into the dark-garbed figure he surprised in the back yard. He felt a sharp sting on his forehead, but ignored it as he struggled with the unbelievably slippery figure. Dull grunts and heavy breathing were the only sounds in the air until his opponent was pinned face down on the ground, his arm yanked behind his back. Jake pressed upward. "Stop struggling," he bit out, "or I'll break it."

"Ow! If you break my arm, Jake Stefani, so help me, I'll never speak to you again!"

The distinctly feminine voice startled him into easing back his grip. He yanked his intruder up into the light at the side of the house. "Carrie! What the hell are you doing here?" His voice boomed over the furious thrumming of his pulse.

"I was trying to get your attention," she yelled back, her fists on her hips.

Bewildered by her behavior, his pleasure at seeing her, Jake was speechless. Grabbing her by the hand, he led her inside the house. Riker was just as thrilled to see her. The dog jumped between them, wagged his tail, kissed her over and over. When Riker dug his claws in the top of Jake's shoeless foot to get to Carrie, he finally had the presence of mind to speak a command to make the dog sit.

Without the animal impeding the way, Jake sat Carrie down on the sofa and turned on a light. He stood over her, his anger at the danger she'd placed herself in taking precedence over the swirl of other emotions. "You've got my attention now, Carrie." He didn't know whether to kiss her senseless or shake her for scaring him so badly. "Do you want to explain that insanity outside?"

"I just did." Her chin lifted. "I rang the doorbell, but you didn't answer. When I remembered it was broken, your bedroom window was my next best option. How was I supposed to know the glass was so fragile?"

Her gaze swept over him from his bare feet to his

equally naked chest. "If you want to talk about insanity, let's discuss why you rushed out to confront what you thought was an intruder with only your good looks to protect you."

"My good —"

Jake moaned and dropped onto the sofa beside her, his head in his hands. Carrie set him on fire and rattled his brains. He raised his head to tell her so, opened his mouth, and promptly shut it.

Carrie had paled alarmingly. "Oh no, you're hurt. Why didn't you tell me?"

"Of course, I'm hurt! What the hell did you think would happen when you left me?" It was wrong to shout at her but what did she expect?

Riker whined at his raised voice and left his post to stand next to Carrie. "Good boy," Jake said, glad the dog was so protective of the woman he loved.

Carrie ruffled Riker's fur behind his ears to reassure him. When he settled at her feet, she reached out to Jake. Her fingertips smoothed across his forehead and came back into view stained with blood. "Jake, you're hurt," she said softly. "I never meant to hurt you."

The tears glistening on her lashes did it. Helpless to stop himself, Jake dragged her into his lap. "It's all right, honey. It's only a scratch." He cuddled her before putting space between them again. "Okay, so what was so important it couldn't wait until daylight? Why are you here?"

With one look at her fingertips, she lifted her hand. "This is why."

Startled, he laughed. "You came over to draw blood?"

She glared at him. "That's not funny."

He sighed. "Tell me."

Carrie told him about her discussion with Eric and her trip downtown. "You were right. Life is too short, too unpredictable to control. I never planned to fall in love again. But, I did. I stepped out into the open and I can't go back. I want to live with you every day and love you every night."

Her voice cracked. "I'm stronger with you beside me, Jake." She kissed his unshaven chin. "I don't have to have promises of forever. We'll live each day as it comes. It will be enough." She took a deep breath. "I don't expect you to give up S.W.A.T."

Jake tenderly picked a piece of grass out of her hair. "You're too late. It's one of the things I intended to tell you today. I spoke with my superiors when I returned to work on Monday. As soon as they can recruit and train my replacement, I'm going on reserve."

She frowned. "I can't let you do that, not because of me. Tell them you've changed your mind."

He shook his head. "No. You affected my decision but, I have to admit, Eric and Mateo are the real reasons why I'm looking at other options."

"I'm confused."

"I was questioning my place on the team long before I met you and Eric. My entire career has been about catching the bad guys and serving justice. But then, I met Mateo Reyes in my old neighborhood. He was a good kid, just misguided and unsure of himself. I tried for months to help him but I failed him."

"You can't blame yourself."

"I've accepted my part in what happened," he said. He picked up her hand and stroked his thumb over her soft skin. Just touching her gave him peace. "It doesn't change the fact that I was too late to help the Reyes brothers after they were embedded in the gang. If I'd gotten to them sooner, I might have had a greater impact on their lives. As it is, I have to be satisfied with only saving one of them."

Carrie looked into his eyes. "One of them? You found Julio?"

"He found me." Jake smiled, still not believing all that had taken place the past seventy-two hours. "He knew his days were numbered when he betrayed the gang to the drug task force, so he's been in deep hiding for the past four months."

"That's why no one could find him."

Jake nodded. "He was afraid of exposing his family to repercussions so he didn't attempt to contact them. When he finally poked his head up, he heard through the grapevine that I was looking for him and called his mother. She told him what happened to Mateo and the rest is history.

"He called me, determined to help take down the gang once and for all. I brought him in and he started spilling Dragons' secrets to the gang task force, right down to where the bodies are buried. They're still sifting through his information, but they've arrested a couple dozen gangbangers including their leader, shut down two major drug operations, and reopened three cold case murders. You'll be hearing about it in the news for the next few weeks as they sort it all out."

She stroked a finger over the new lines around his eyes. "This is why you're looking so tired."

"It's been a wild week," Jake agreed.

Only part of his exhaustion could be chalked up to the events of the past few days though. He was looking at the biggest reason he'd barely slept since Saturday. When he wasn't involved in the details of his job or supporting Julio and his mother, he was thinking about Carrie.

He drank up the sight of her luscious caramel eyes. His fingers played with her cinnamon hair lying over her breast. He felt the comforting weight of her body lying across his thighs, in the circle of his arms again. Finally. Unable to wait any longer, Jake did what he'd been dying to do since finding Carrie in his backyard holding a sharp rock and an even sharper attitude. He kissed her. Long. Hard. With each caress, he erased the harsh memories of their separation.

When his mouth lifted from hers, they were both breathing hard. Jake chuckled dryly. "Maybe I'd better finish this explanation before I can't."

"Explanation?"

Carrie looked as confused as he felt. "We were talking about my career. Why I'm leaving S.W.A.T."

"Oh." She blinked. "Right."

Jake cleared his throat. "My superiors were right to force me on vacation. It forced me to think about my career choices. Somewhere along the way, I took a wrong turn. I've spent the past nine years addressing policing problems after they've become an issue, not before. I threw hours at it, instead of hitting it head on. When my restlessness got worse, I took on S.W.A.T., too. These past weeks with Eric and his friends made me realize my dissatisfaction wouldn't go away until I got back to the real issues that bothered me. I want to work with kids, get to them before they make bad decisions that can destroy them and their families."

"How will you do that?"

"There's a program, sort of a junior police corps, which involves training kids in police procedures directing them down the right side of the law. It never really got off the ground when it was launched several years ago. I've convinced my superiors to give me a shot at getting it up and running. It would be a parallel program to the school district's anti-drug program already in place."

Carrie's hand stroked his jaw. "Sounds like something you'd be good at. You're wonderful with Eric and the other kids."

He turned his head to kiss her palm, then placed it over his naked chest where he wanted it. "I'm still a cop, Carrie. Police work is what I do. It's what I am. You've got to be sure that you can live with that. I can't be worrying about how you'll react every time I walk out the door."

She sighed, her fingertips playing with the hair over his heart. "I can't say I won't worry about you, Jake, because it wouldn't be true. I love you. It's only natural to worry about the people you love, isn't it?"

Jake cleared his throat, trying to keep his mind on what she was saying, not what she was doing with her fingers. "As long as it doesn't control your life."

Carrie dragged her knuckles down to his flat stomach and back up again. "I haven't had any control since the day I met you." She placed her mouth against the hot skin above his breastbone.

He groaned deep in his throat, his voice rusty. "I guess I'll have to do something about that. It is my job to keep crazed women off the streets of Riverton." His hands separated her navy shirt from the waistband of her jeans. His breath caught when he uncovered the heated flesh at the base of her spine.

"You'd better get busy then." She twisted in his lap and kissed him, her tongue darting into his mouth, retreating. Teasing. Tantalizing. "Because I am crazy, my love," she said. "Crazy about you."

It took him a long while to say anything with her lips in the way. "You do realize that I have no choice but to put you under house arrest," he said when he came up for air. "After all, you did vandalize my house and I do have your confession."

She laughed. "I told you I didn't mean to do that."

"Explain it to the judge."

Her smile faltered. "What judge?"

"The one in Vail that will marry us. You'll put me out of my misery quickly, won't you?" His lips curved. "Mama's threatened to come up here with Sophia Mazzini."

Carrie sat back and scowled. "She sounds tall, curvaceous and hot-blooded."

"She's short, fat, and cold as a mackerel. But she's single, I'm single, and Mama's determined to have her bambinos. I don't have a choice." Jake shrugged. "I've called in a few favors to arrange for a four-day weekend in Vail in three weeks. I've rented a friend's condo on the side of the mountain, which is a ten minute walk to an outdoor retreat at the top that specializes in weddings. The only question is whom I'm taking with me. It's either you or Sophia Mazzini."

"You're pretty sure of yourself, aren't you? What if I can't get off work? Sam's offered me the Berthoud office and I don't think he—"

"You're talking about the man who told Eric that you needed a man to take care of you, right?"

She laughed at the reminder of the first time they'd met. "If I didn't love you so much—"

With one hand tangled in her hair, the other sliding up her back, Jake kissed her. She felt giddy by the time he finished. "You were saying?"

Carrie cleared her throat and whispered. "I think I was saying 'yes'. What's-her-name can rent her own condo."

"Good." He kissed her nose and nuzzled the sensitive chord of her neck. "Um. Do you think Eric would mind coming home a week early?"

It was difficult to concentrate on the question, but she felt a slight thrill to think about Eric's reaction to their news. "He'll come back tomorrow, if you ask him."

"We'll call him later today and give him the news, but let's give him time with his grandparents while we have a proper honeymoon."

She tried to look scandalized. "You're planning the honeymoon before the wedding?"

He grinned and rose to his feet, taking her with him. "You want to have a honeymoon *after* Eric gets home?"

When she shook her head and moved to lower her feet to the floor, he jockeyed her higher. "Oh no, you don't," he said, his voice thickening with desire. "You, lady, are under house arrest."

"Jake!" Carrie laughed when she saw where they were headed. Riker ran alongside them like it was a new game he wanted to play. "What's the sentence, Officer Stefani?"

He stopped halfway up the stairs to look into her eyes. "Life."

It was a good thing he held her to his heart because she could have melted down the stairs at the intense look on his face. "I love you so much, Jake, I'll take what I can get."

With a sudden grin, he ran the rest of the way up the stairs and entered his bedroom. Then, he kicked the door shut in Riker's face. The dog was so startled, he didn't even bark.

Walking across the room Jake laid her on the bed, slid in behind her, and gathered her back into his arms. "I love you, too, honey. I want to spend a lifetime proving it to you." His kiss was searching, both a demand and a promise.

Carrie snuggled deeper into his embrace. "Jake?"

"Hmmm?"

"This house arrest," she moaned, wriggling against his hard length, "do you have to be a policeman or can just anyone do it?"

Jake's groan vibrated through her body as he tucked her beneath him and framed her face in his large hands. His hot chocolate eyes glowed with a steady fire that she knew would never go out. "It doesn't matter," he said, lowering his head to brush her lips with his. "I surrender."

Books By Karen

Subscribe to my blog at http://www.karendocter.com/ for a chance to win one $5 Amazon or Starbucks gift card (winner's choice) each month. All subscribers will be included in the monthly drawing.

Contemporary Romance by Karen Docter:
Satin Pleasures
Catch That Santa (Novellette)

Romantic Suspense by K.L. Docter
Killing Secrets (A Thorne's Thorns Novel)

True Love In Uniform (Contemporary Romance)
Cop On Her Doorstep
Cop Crashes The Wedding (Coming Soon)

Karen Docter

Copyright

245